He tilted her head to touch her lips with his, softly at first, then with more urgency, more warmth, until Lyndell's very soul melted. And yet . . . and yet she was a lady. She wasn't any lightskirt to be tumbled in the hay. She wasn't any mousey old spinster either. She was, for the first time in days, Miss Lyndell Markham, a lady.

She took one step away, drew back her arm, and smashed him across the cheek with every ounce of strength her outrage lent her.

"Just who in blazes do you think you are?" she spit out.

MY LADY INNKEEPER

Barbara Metzger

FAWCETT CREST • NEW YORK

A Fawcett Crest Book
Published by Ballantine Books
Copyright © 1985 by Barbara Metzger

Library of Congress Catalog Card Number: 84-19635

ISBN 0-449-21882-1

Manufactured in the United States of America

First Ballantine Books Edition: July 1990

When I was little, my grandfather would call my sister by her name, Carole. He also called me Carole. When we were together, he'd say, Hi Carole, who's your friend?

This one's for Carole, anyway. With love.

Chapter One

"Toads! All men are toads," declared Miss Lyndell Markham as she paced around her aunt's sitting room, waving a scrap of parchment. "They seek a woman for her money, her family name, her looks or her virtue—not an honest motive in their hearts. A woman can't trust any of them!" Miss Markham paused in her agitation to seek confirmation from her audience of one, her cousin Isabelle, whose advanced state of pregnancy proclaimed her trafficking with the enemy. Bella murmured "No, dear," without missing a stitch of her embroidery. Miss Markham's complaints were not new ones. Nor were they without foundation.

Unfortunately for man's baser motives, Miss Markham was blessed, or cursed, with a multitude of temptations. As for wealth, she was one of the foremost heiresses of the realm; for lineage, the sole child of the late Earl of Markham, whose title was ancient and impeccable. As to beauty, with her vibrant red-gold hair now cropped into fashionable curls, startlingly clear green eyes, a peach-blush complexion and a graceful figure of ideal proportions, the whole carried with an elegance of manner and garbed in exquisite taste, Lyndell just missed perfection by a nose. The Markham Nose, to be exact; patrician to be polite; less than straight to be truthful. As her father had predicted, "As long as my money is inherited with my nose, they'll still call her a Beauty." If not an Incomparable, she was often called the Magnificent Miss Markham.

As for virtue, in certain baser circles, such as White's betting book, she was dubbed the Unmountable Markham. Lyndell had managed to attain her twenty-fourth year with virtue intact despite importunities by every expert with rakish ways and roving hands. These importunities provided one, but only one, of the day's grievances. In a swirl of amber crepe and green riband, Lyndell flicked the letter at her inattentive cousin.

"It's not enough I have to suffer every puppy's drooling and every basket-scrambler's begging to pay his addresses—to my estate!—but now every loose screw feels I've been on the Town so long I'm past the age of innocence."

With a faint smile, Isabelle denied the possibility. "Come, Lyndy, no gentleman would treat you like a . . . a . . ."

"A lightskirt? Bella, you are such a babe! Yes, I know you're an old married woman of twenty-six. But you're a prelate's wife." Before Isabelle could make any disclaimers, Lyndell recommenced her pacing, her steps the strides of a tall, confident woman. "Here, do you know Lord Naybors?"

"Yes, I met his wife at—"

"Last night at the Bellinghams' ball he asked me

2

to stand up with him and I accepted, thinking to have some rational conversation at last. He kept dancing toward the balconies and then almost pushed me out, for some fresh air, he said."

"But Lyndy, it was freezing! It's November!"

"Exactly! And his wife is at home with a sick child! I put a flea in his ear, you can be sure, but it's always the same. Society says a woman's reputation is all-important, and every man is out to help her lose it. Then she'll be labelled 'fast,' Society will turn its back, and no one will marry her! Well, I am tired of those games."

"Is there no man who can inspire a *tendre* in you?"

"What, Bella, you too?"

Isabelle flushed and lowered her eyes to her needlework again, fashioning rosebuds to an impossibly tiny bonnet.

"Are you joining the throng to see me wed? Aunt and Uncle are despairing, and even Lady Jersey hinted I was too long in the tooth to be so particular."

"No, Lyndy, you know I only want to see you happy!" Bella didn't say, "As I am," and Lyndell didn't say, "Married to an old stick as you are?" but she gave an unladylike snort. "Not likely, among the lobcocks and loobies one sees at all the *Ton* parties. I've met all the eligibles, and I'd rather stay on the shelf!"

"Perhaps Father could speak to an older gentleman, one with wealth of his own . . . ?"

"You mean a marriage of convenience? I think not! I've found them to be damnably inconvenient, especially for the woman! She gives up her freedom, hands her finances into his keeping, in exchange for what? The right to bear his children!

3

The husband now has her properties to gamble away without touching his own holdings, and the right, no, the responsibility, to enjoy his mistresses in Town, while his wife sits in the country breeding. No, thank you!"

"But, Lyndy, don't you wish to be married at all?"

There was a moment of silence as Lyndell seemed to lose some of her bravado. She sank to the floor near her cousin's chair, fingering the tiny cap.

"Yes, Bella." She spoke in a subdued tone, and with a tinge of wistful sadness. "I would dearly like to be married, to love and be loved, to *share*. But I cannot give my hand without giving my heart, and I've not found the man I could love and trust and . . . and cherish, the way my parents did each other. Do you understand, cousin, that I could never do what Mama did, after Papa died? I may stay on the shelf forever, but I'll never marry just so I'll not be alone."

Lady Markham's second marriage, a scant year after the earl's passing, was a mistake, and a further tragedy for the grieving twelve-year-old Lyndell. She simply couldn't understand how her sweet, gentle mother could transfer her affections from the Earl of Markham, a noble in every respect, to the very common Joshua Riddley. It was not that the young Miss Markham was a snob, but Riddley was far beneath her father in education, civility, gentility, everything that makes for a cultured gentleman. In fact, Riddley was no gentleman. A member of the most minor landed gentry, his main interests were gaming, drinking and riding to the hounds. When he couldn't chase the fox, he chased serving girls. This was the man Lyndell's mother chose to succeed the earl. Despite capable managers and her own brother's assistance, Lady Markham simply could not face the responsibilities of the vast King's Mark estate and a willful daughter, combined with the bleak future of years of loneliness ahead, or having to face the London Marriage Mart as a no-longer-young widow. And there was Joshua Riddley, a widower with a young son. He was jovial, undemanding, known for years; he was ready to shoulder all her burdens.

If Lady Markham's burdens were the sweetest windfall Riddley had ever known, he managed to hide his true colours. At least for a few months after the wedding, that is, until he saw exactly what was his directly, through his wife's settlements, and what he could carefully glean as overseer of the earl's unentailed properties—Lyndell's inheritance. Suddenly he could indulge his habits to excesses he had only dreamt of, embarrassing his new wife, infuriating and mortifying his new daughter. He abused the servants, misused or neglected the tenants and the lands Lyndell had been taught to honour; he used Markham money to set his own son Jasper up as a wastrel, a fribble with no need to earn a living or learn a trade, just another gaming, drinking leech.

Neither father nor son had the mental scope to beggar the estate nor, with the capital investments untouchable in London, to greatly affect Lyndell's wealth, yet the lands, and her pride, suffered. For four years she could do nothing. Then her mother died. Faded, tired, isolated by embarrassment from all social life, Mrs. Riddley drifted from weakness to illness to death. It was, or seemed to the then sixteen-year-old Lyndell, another solution of least effort, another betrayal. Before leaving King's Mark to take up residence with her Aunt Lillian and Uncle Hardesty in London, Lyndell threw the Riddleys off her lands. The father she threatened with court action if he ever approached her again. To her step-brother Jasper, an ineffectual ne'er-do-well, she offered a one-time sum of money to purchase an army commission, or passage to America, or a university education so he might find a profession, whatever, just to be gone. Now, eight years later, after the Bath Seminary for Young Ladies, after her presentation and warm welcome to the *Ton*, Lyndell still carried the scars of distrust and disdain.

Today she also carried a letter from Jasper Riddley.

Shaking off the despondency of sad memories and loss, Lyndell jumped to her feet and tossed her head, as if to rearrange her thoughts along with her curls. Laughing, she proclaimed, "Men are all fools. They must inherit it from their fathers!"

Isabelle was relieved at the lightening of her cousin's mood and hastened to change the topic. "I collect you mean Jasper—you said he'd written—but I can't understand what has you in such a taking. He is not asking for more money, is he? I thought that was settled years ago."

"Oh yes, well settled! I paid his debts and thought to provide for his future in some respectable way. Instead he and Joshua went to London and proceeded to gamble the sum away. If Joshua hadn't been killed in a duel over some marked cards, they would both have landed in debtor's prison, and I'd have let them rot there."

"You know you wouldn't have been so hard, Lyndy, especially not on poor Jasper."

" 'Poor Jasper,' is it? You always had a soft spot for him, even as a child, after he rescued your kitten from the goldfish pond. I always thought he'd tossed it in himself just to tease you, but no mind. I don't know if I actually could have let Jasper die in prison, but I would certainly have let him sit there a while. It might have averted his next actions."

"You mean the inn?"

"Yes. To take what remained of his money—my money!—and return to Suffolk, not ten minutes away from King's Mark, and purchase a tavern! Not even a respectable coaching house on the Norwich road where he might have made a profit, but a dreary little wayside inn, little more than a hedgerow pub. And he had the nerve, the sheer gall, to call it King's Pass!"

Isabelle smiled. "Perhaps he was acknowledging his debt to you."

Lyndell merely gave her cousin a dark look. "It never mattered overmuch, since no one in London knew of the relation, and everyone near home knew I had cut the connexion, but my . . . my . . . stepbrother"—the words almost choked her—"a common innkeep! And none too successful either. His principal income came from fleecing at cards any well-heeled traveller unfortunate enough to be stranded at the place. If he could. More often Jasper would lose. The noddy couldn't even cheat right! But that's nothing, nothing, I tell you, to this! Here." She handed the letter over to her cousin. "See for yourself."

" 'Dear Sister,' " Isabelle read, ignoring the unladylike growl coming from Lyndell's throat. 'Here is the deed to King's Pass Inn, made over to your name. No fear, they'll never connect you with the spies.' Oh dear."

"It gets better. Keep reading."

"'I swear to you I thought the Quinns, the previous owners, you know—they stayed on to run the inn for me—were merely involved with the Gentlemen. That's smugglers, if you don't know the term. But it turns out they were also waylaying couriers bound for the army installations at Southwold Barracks, drugging the wine and copying orders, or getting the soldiers jug-bitten enough to tell secrets, and passing the information on to the Frenchies, with the help of some London swell. The messengers would never reveal they'd stopped off for a wet, or a wench, so no one was the wiser till a courier was found dead and his papers gone, and a Captain Drew Jamison started nosing around. The Quinns shabbed off, leaving me in a pretty pickle, I can tell you. Quinn said his London connexion—it could have been any of several nobs who stopped here occasionally—would be watching to make sure I didn't snabble on them or they'd dim my lights too.'"

Bella looked up enquiringly.

"That means kill him," Lyndell informed her tersely.

After a quick horrified gasp, Bella continued to read: "'With Nappy defeated the whole should blow over eventually unless the magistrates connect me somehow to the dead messenger, or to a few robberies at the coaching inn by Framingham. Then I'd be finished either way, so I'm hiding out for a while. Dilly, I'm depending on you to save my skin. Yours too, if it comes to that. You wouldn't want your brother up on King's Bench warrants, I'm sure. I know you can pull it off with all your influence in Town. You're my only hope. Your affectionate brother, Jasper.'" Isabelle's voice faded away, as she sat in stunned silence.

"Spies, smugglers, highwaymen. What do you think of Jasper now? I'll bet he knew all along what was going on. Even a skitterwit like Riddley can recognise French brandy and despatch cases. As long as he was being paid, he'd not question the French Army's landing force putting up at his miserable inn! And how true to character, running off, leaving me with a witches' broth abrewing!" Spots of colour highlighted Miss Markham's cheeks as her redheaded temper again took control.

"But Lyndy, what are you going to do?"

"Do?" she sputtered. "What should I do? Run to the Admiralty and say my step-brother knows a spy in London but he's too cowardly to identify him, so please forgive him? Or tell the magistrate Jasper would never exert himself so far as to murder anyone, but he's simply gone on a repairing lease, so you must not suspect him? What kind of fool would I look?"

"Good heavens," Isabelle said as it all sank in, "He'll be deported, giving aid and shelter to criminals."

"Oh, no, he won't." Lyndell countered, "They hang traitors."

Chapter Two

Inactivity and indecision made up no part of Lyndell Markham's five-foot-six-inch frame. Having taken control of her own life at the age of sixteen, and capably too, she was not about to yield her fate to mere chance now. Especially with the London Season growing so tedious, and what looked to be high adventure beckoning. Murder, mayhem, treason, a high-born villain—the Minerva Press couldn't equal Jasper's bumblebath. Lyndell knew exactly what she had to do: leave London with as little fanfare as possible, set herself up at the inn, and trap the spy. The details could be worked out later.

The first part of the plan involved swearing Isabelle to cooperative secrecy. From years of experience with her headstrong cousin, Isabelle knew better than to try dissuading Lyndell from her hey-go-mad start, but she did inject some practicality by mentioning such items as danger and propriety.

It was unthinkable for a well-born lady to be staying at an inn unchaperoned, and everyone within miles of King's Mark would recognise the earl's daughter. Furthermore, what could a single woman do in the face of such ruthlessness that Jasper couldn't? Lyndell was forced to agree that her plan had flaws, but with a little thought she could correct the major problems: first, she would pretend to be Miss Lynn Riddley, Jasper's sister and the new innkeeperess, and she would wear a disguise, which, to Isabelle's dismay, seemed to make the plot even more attractive. Lyndell would stay away from her home, and take no London servants who could gossip. Instead she'd ask the Bennetts to travel with her, for protection and to satisfy convention. Sarah Bennett had been Lyndell's nurserymaid and Joseph had been her father's groom. Pensioned off to a cottage in Islington, there was no more respectable, loyal pair. Isabelle had to be content.

Lady Hardesty was even easier for Lyndell to persuade, by the simple expedient of lying. Miss Markham appeased her conscience by reflecting that the truth would only worry Aunt Lillian, and what way was that to repay all her kindnesses? Besides, Lyndell had to start practicing subterfuge somewhere, if she was to be any good at thief-taking. So she claimed a serious problem at the manor—not far from the truth—and exhaustion from the constant London rounds, as her reasons for begging off all their engagements. If Lady Hardesty was a little quick in her acceptance of Lyndell's departure, Lyndell could understand. It could be no pleasure for Aunt Lillian either, despite the many disclaimers, to be still chaperoning her niece after all these years, listening to the tattle-mongers link Lyndell's name with one bachelor after another, and have the girl still, disappointingly, on her hands. After all, Lady Hardesty had married her own daughter off before Bella was eighteen. Of course, she'd often said, it was different; Lyndell was an heiress. But no, as long as she knew the Bennetts were along, Aunt Lillian could see no objection to the Suffolk trip.

The Bennetts, however, were not so easy to convince.

Lyndell straightened the bow on her chip-straw bonnet as the carriage drew up before the neat white cottage with its kitchen garden off to the side. She had to laugh at herself, a grown woman, tidying up to face people who'd known her as an infant. That they still shared a comfortable affection was obvious in the warm greetings, the cosy hominess of tea and fresh-baked strawberry tarts in the tiny kitchen. There could be no untruths here, Lyndell knew, not when she was asking them to share the danger. A little subtlety, perhaps, but no outright lies.

"Do you remember the inn Jasper Riddley purchased, just to the south of King's Mark?" she asked, after the table had been cleared and Bennett's clay pipe had been lit. "The one the Quinns used to have?"

At their nods she continued, "Well, Jasper's run into a bit of difficulty and I wish to go there to see what help I can be. And it occurred to me you might enjoy a holiday in the country as well."

"How nice for you to think of us, dear, wasn't it, Mr. Bennett?"

Joseph raised one brow and thoughtfully tapped his pipe on the fireplace.

"Then again," Lyndell continued, figuring in for

12

a pence, in for a pound. "I'm fairly certain Jasper will be removing from the area permanently and I thought you might be interested in taking over the inn." She had an awful moment of self-reflection when she saw herself enmeshed in the life of crime: cajolery, then lies, now bribery, and she'd only been at it for a few hours! What next? Go for the weak spot! She turned to Sarah. "You know you've been saying how the city is getting so large it'll be at your doorstep soon, with all its noise and dirt and bother. And you, Benny, I know you'd rather keep horses of your own than work for hire at that livery, and you'd still have your pensions. I thought we could all travel together, and stay a short while to see if you like it, before making any decisions. Of course we'd have to start out soon."

Bennett's dour "of course" received an answering twinkle from Lyndell, but Mrs. Bennett was enthusiastic. "Just think, Mr. Bennett, a big garden and fresh country air and good, honest folks, all in visiting distance of King's Mark." She looked around and lowered her voice. "I shouldn't be saying this to you, Miss Lyndy, but Islington is getting Fast. It is too, Mr. Bennett, don't you laugh. That little house at the corner, the one with the nice primroses, was sold last month to Lord Ainsley—and for what? To house his . . . his . . . oh dear."

Lyndell smiled, showing a dimple, and patted Sarah's hand. "All the more reason to consider a move. What do you think, Benny?"

His wife looked at him anxiously but Mr. Bennett only studied the tobacco in the pipe, poking at it and puffing, before turning to Lyndell at last. "This bit o'difficulty young Riddley found himself in, just what might that be?"

Flushing slightly, and lowering her eyes, Lyndell

told them about the letter, all of it, and her plan to clear Jasper's name and safeguard her own, with their help. "It's not that we'd be so all alone, either. There's this Captain Jamison, and the whole King's Mark staff if we need it."

"It's not quite what I'd like," Mrs. Bennett confessed. "You pretending to be what you're not, and people not like to treat you as a Lady of Quality, but we're good loyal Englishmen too, aren't we, Joseph?"

Bennett thought he knew enough about traitors to be fairly sure none would return to a scene of so much suspicion, so he hadn't many misgivings on that score. He also thought he knew enough about young creatures, horses or otherwise, to probe a little deeper. "Won't you be missin' out on all those fine parties and such? The missus'n I could go on and see what's in the wind, without you comin' along."

Lyndell almost squeaked, "Without me? Oh no! What are a few parties—they're all so boring anyhow, after the first few—compared to this? I wouldn't miss it for anything!" When she noted Bennett's grin, she added, "And don't you start on me about wasting time when I could be finding a husband, either. I'd rather catch a spy!"

"But, dear," Sarah started, looking from one to the other, before she was interrupted by her husband's muttered, "The gypsy fair again."

"What was that, Mr. Bennett?" she asked, but Lyndell was blushing, a curse of her fair skin.

Bennett had to pause to relight his pipe. "The gypsy fair. Miss Lyndy was nobut six years or so, and I was undergroom. Th'earl and Henesley were off buyin' horses and little miss here, red hair in braids down her back, 'n no front teeth, comes up'n tells me to saddle her pony, she's goin' to the gypsy fair. So I asks if the earl said she could and she tells me he didn't say she couldn't."

"Well, he didn't," Lyndell put in.

"Then she says she'll go anyway, if I don't help her creep out where no one's lookin', because she has two pence all her own and wants to have her fortune told. I wasn't going to saddle up that pony no how, but she looks up at me with those green eyes all watery and a quiver in her voice, sayin' she'll be my friend, forever, if I go with her. I was cotched, all right and tight. That little grey pony—"

"Peasblossom."

"—barely come up to my stirrups, but Missy sat so tall in her saddle, off adventuring."

"And a fine adventure it was, too, Benny."

"Until we got home. Henesley wanted to have my hide, but the earl, he understood."

"Understood? Gammon, I couldn't sit for a week!"

"He told me there'd always be women who could wrap men around their little fingers—like his puss, he called her—and there'd always be men spineless enough to curl up tight for them. Like me, I guess. Inevitable, is what he called it. And he weren't mad, just so's long as I kept her safe." He stared at his wife, then grinned. "So when are we off to the gypsy fair?"

It wasn't till Lyndell's fine carriage had pulled away, plans made, times set, that Sarah said to her husband, "Adventuring indeed. That girl needs a husband," and he answered, "Amen to that."

Chapter Three

$\mathcal{A}$fter an early morning start, they changed carriages at the posting house in Chelmsford, the first stage out of London, so as not to inconvenience Lord Hardesty any further, Lyndell told her uncle's driver. It looked like snow, and she didn't wish the coach and horses stranded in the country. If the London servants thought it too smoky by half for Miss not to be driven direct to her destination, they were too used to the ways of the Quality to be bothered overmuch, and Bennett's largesse also helped quiet their reservations, and their tongues.

So Mrs. Bennett and Lyndell, the hood of her green cloak pulled over the unmistakable coppery curls, her head lowered, were shown into a private parlour while Joseph Bennett hired a chaise to continue their journey. At the next stages, Lyndell and Sarah stayed in the coach while the horses were changed, an unremarkable young woman and her companion, taking refreshment from the hamper at their feet. It wasn't till just past Framingham, well into Suffolk, that any change occurred. First Lyndell opened her cloak and laid it aside to reveal a grey merino gown of fairly good quality, but with no embellishments to mark it a fashionable creation. It had a loose enough fit to hide Lyndell's own notable figure and at the same time proclaim to the experienced eye that Miss Lynn Riddley bought ready-made clothing. Serviceable and unpretentious, the grey merino, along with a dreary brown bombazine and a plain navy kerseymere hidden under Lyndell's muslins and silks, was Isabelle's prepregnancy visit-the-poor clothes. From the portmanteau at her feet Lyndell next pulled a huge droopy nightcap, a relic of Isabelle's mother-in-law's last visit. Unlike the scraps of lace most ladies perched on their heads to denote their attaining "a certain age," this item more closely resembled a dairymaid's mob-cap—after the cow had worn it too. It did have the advantage of hiding every stray curl of Lyndell's hair, and, flopping over her brow as it did, of shadowing the sparkle in her green eyes. Right now those eyes were alight with merriment as she pulled from her reticule a pair of spectacles, Uncle Hardesty's unknowing contribution, and placed them low on the bridge of her nose, right at the Markham deviation. A touch of powder to dull her fine complexion, a slight stoop to the shoulders, and voilà, Miss Lynn Riddley, spinster. Poor but respectable, meekly come to hold house or inn for her brother. What a great actress she would be, Lyndell decided, if she ever got tired of the *Ton*.

Unfortunately, there was no one but the hired driver and his postillion to behold her performance, and they had seen nothing more than the green cape before. Instead of being impressed by her

17

transformation, or even noticing it, they wished only to discharge their passengers and head back toward Chelmsford while some grey afternoon light still remained. And before the snow started.

Bennett's knee-slapping guffaws almost compensated, but there was no mistaking that her grand entrance was marred by the lack of an audience. The place was deserted. A dog barked somewhere, the only sign of life, so Lyndell took the spectacles off before she tripped, straightened up to help tote parcels in, and jauntily set off to inspect her new surroundings.

The tavern sign, a faded blue horse running, hung crookedly. Someone, Jasper most likely, had crudely painted a crowned figure on the horse's back. The King, passing by, as any sane customer would do. The inn's exterior was something less than dramatic; it was dingy. A two-story brick-and-beam construction, it hadn't so much as a single rosebush to relieve the dreariness. The inside was no better. The large common room smelled of stale ale and staler bodies. The one tiny private parlour was dark, and showed none too clean in what weak light filtered through the smoke-grimed windows. To the rear were the kitchen, a nearly empty pantry, a few minute rooms for maidservants, and what must have been the Quinns' quarters. . . . They'd left the bed and the wash stand.

"How nice," Mrs. Bennett declared firmly. "We'll have lots of room for our rugs and furniture from Islington. If we decide to stay, of course."

Lyndell was doubtful. "There's a great deal of work to be done . . ."

"And best it got started. I just knew you'd ought to have a lady's maid with you. 'Tisn't proper, no one to bring you hot water to wash. Well, there's no hot water either. You, Mr. Bennett, go find the woodpile and see to lighting some fires while I air these rooms and check the stores, so's we can have some tea. Things'll look better with some warm food in us. And Joseph, the trunk and that hamper . . ."

Lyndell escaped upstairs, travelling case in hand.

At the top of the stairs the corridor branched to left and right, with doors showing on either side of the hall. The opened rooms were tiny, but at least neat, waiting for the occasional merchant or family travelling to Yarmouth, Lyndell supposed. They were certainly nowhere as fine as the least grand room she'd ever stayed in, so *any* noble putting up here was either down on his luck, lost, or a suspect. Selecting the right-hand corridor and wishing she'd brought a candle, Lyndell continued on till she found Jasper's apartments at the end of the hall. A small sitting room and the bedroom beyond had his unmistakable stamp: clothes strewn all over, racing papers and playing cards spilling from the bureau, empty bottles guarding the corners, an article of feminine apparel dangling from a wall sconce. Definitely Jasper's rooms. She carefully sidestepped piles of papers and account books, deciding to leave it all untouched till she could make an organised search for any hints Jasper might have left. Another bedroom opened off the sitting room—for Jasper's lady callers?—and this Lyndell selected for her own use. It was clean and dry and convenient for her investigation, and logical for Jasper's "sister." By the light of a candle finally located, Lyndell unpacked a few of her belongings, straightened the cap over her curls and repowdered her face. Her grumbling stomach taking precedence over immediate exploration of the left-hand corridor, Lyndell returned to the kitchen, where she found Mrs. Bennett bustling over kettles and a welcome fire.

"Tea will be ready in a minute, dear. I've just been making lists for Mr. Bennett to fetch from market, if the snow holds off for him to drive tomorrow. Jasper left his carriage—there's a dray for supplies, and some horses—Joseph is seeing to them now. Why don't you fetch him?"

The cold wind was blowing leaves about as Lyndell hurried across the rear yard. With her head down and one hand holding on to her cap, she almost came too close to a huge dog chained to a post. Its low snarls warned her when she was just outside its lunge distance, as she quickly found out. Saying "Good doggie, nice doggie," to a creature showing foot-long fangs made Lyndell feel like a fool, but the animal went back to a pile of meat— probably its previous owner, Lyndell decided. Eyeing her warily, but not as warily as she eyed it, the dog ate while Lyndell edged toward the stables.

"You could have warned me about that dog, Benny," she called into the dark reaches of the barn.

"Didn't know you was comin', did I?" he answered as he backed out of a stall dragging a bundle of . . . sticks? Rags? "I got it some food from the missus, but there's no getting near it. Prob'ly have to shoot the poor beast in the mornin'." At those words whatever he was holding made a noise a lot like the dog's and dashed for the stable door, right into Lyndell's arms.

"Why, it's a boy!" she exclaimed. She could see the tatters he was wearing and feel the skinny arm trembling, but she only heard those animal-like noises when she asked his name and what he was doing there.

"He don't talk much, it seems, but he must've took care of the horses when Jasper left. There's plenty of grain and hay. Not much for a boy or a dog, what I can see. Best take him to the missus. C'mon, lad, we'll get some warm food in you."

Lyndell wasn't taking chances; she held firmly to the small hand, to make sure he didn't escape, she told herself. The boy might also be a safe passage through the chained beast's territory, herself added, honest to a fault.

There was still another surprise waiting in the kitchen, one more of Jasper's bequeathals. If the authorities didn't hang him, Lyndell decided, she would, gladly.

Sarah made the introductions: "Miss Lynn Riddley, this is Molly. She says she's serving girl in the tap room."

As Molly bobbed an awkward curtsy, her . . . endowments . . . nearly bobbing out of the low-cut blouse, it was all too easy to see just what Molly served to the customers. The rouged cheeks and impossibly yellow hair proclaimed her no better than she ought to be, and probably a lot worse.

Surprisingly, it was Joseph Bennett who told Molly she might as well stay on, in spite of his wife's sniffing disapproval. "For if you're to cook, Sarah, and I'm to see to the horses, that only leaves Miss Lynn here to see to the customers else." That immediately quieted any protests Mrs. Bennett might have made. Her Miss Lyndy serving ale in a common tap room to a bunch of drunken farmers? She'd see the devil ice-skating first!

"Well, if that's all right and tight I'll just go freshen up," Molly announced. "My room's the end of the other hall from Jasper's, Mr. Riddley, that is, if you need me. With the fires lit and some lan-

21

terns out, maybe we'll have some business tonight."

Lyndell nearly choked with laughter on Molly's unfortunate phrasing, and the look of horror on Sarah's face, but she had to ask about the boy. "Him?" Molly tossed over her shoulder as she flounced out of the kitchen. "He's just the moron Quinn took out of the workhouse to see to the stables."

The boy's growling noises were too much for poor Sarah. She threw her apron over her face and blubbered into it. "A . . . a lightskirt in my own kitchen! Am I to sit to supper with that Jezebel and a lice-ridden, horse-fouled, savage half-wit? I can't do it, Miss Lyndy, I just can't."

Traitor that he was, Bennett went to fetch more wood. Lyndell dragged the boy to a chair near the fire and told him to sit, out of hearing, before returning to pat her old nurse's hand. "There," she said soothingly, "it's just for a while, you know it is! And we can't get rid of Molly. Like Benny said, she has to serve at the tables. She can even eat there, not with us! But she's been here since the Quinns too, so she might have some information."

"I know all about the information women like her have and I don't want her giving any of it to you, you hear me, Miss Lyndy?"

"Of course, Sarah, and I'll stay far away from her, I promise." Lyndell carefully did not promise to stay away from Molly's room, which she intended to search the moment it was unoccupied, if the moment ever came. What she did say was, "But we all have to listen in case she mentions any London gentlemen, or soldiers with important messages. That's what we're here for, remember?" When Sarah nodded, reluctantly, Lyndell went on,

22

lowering her voice still further: "As for the boy, why, he's just cold and hungry and maybe a little dirty. You wouldn't put him out in the snowy night in those rags, with no supper, would you?"

"He took good care of the horses too, Sarah," Bennett added, coming in with a pile of wood and stacking it by the hearth. The boy bent to help him.

"You see, Sarah, he's no savage, just frightened," Lyndell said. "Here," and she took his hand, drawing him to the table near Sarah, where she knelt to his level. "You do understand me, don't you?" The sad little head nodded. "And can you talk if you want to?" A pause, then another nod. "Good! Now, do you have a name?" A vigorous nod. "Of course you do! Well, I am Lyndy, and this is Mrs. Bennett, who is the finest cook anywhere in England. But we have a problem. You see, Mrs. Bennett won't have strangers at her supper table, only friends, and friends always know each other's names so . . ."

A whisper: "Sam'l, ma'am."

"Fine! Well Mrs. Bennett, this is my friend Sam'l, will he do?"

"Of course he will, as soon as Mr. Bennett washes him up some. Here young Sam'l, have some bread and butter to tide you over."

When the boy was shyly nodding his appreciation, Bennett touched his shoulder. "Come on then, Sam'l. I like a lad what doesn't jabber."

By the early suppertime the weather was even more threatening, dark an hour too early, but King's Pass Inn looked almost cosy. Fires had taken the chill off the common room and private parlour, and a quick sweep with a broom had gotten most of the cobwebs. Lyndell's trunk was unpacked and she'd had a warm bath, and a start at Jasper's rooms, though she couldn't have said what she was looking for.

Downstairs, the Bennetts had also unpacked and their rooms looked brighter, with furniture and bedding from one of the unused guest chambers. Sarah and Lyndell had even found an old jacket of Jasper's they cut down for Sam'l—"The least Jasper could contribute"—which they'd sew up later. Scrubbed and fed, warm and dry, he still would not talk much. Lyndell managed to find out that he was eleven, or maybe twelve, and that the dog's name was Ajax—the important things. Sam'l either didn't know or wouldn't say where Jasper was, what he'd been living on these past days, or if any London gentlemen visited frequently. For the most part, Sam'l kept his eyes firmly on his shoes. So much for that source, Lyndell decided, as she sent him off to bed in the stable with the last of Sarah's apple tarts, a pile of warm blankets, and a promise to see about Ajax in the morning. He looked at her, actually *at* her, just for a moment. She thought his eyes were brown; she thought he may have smiled. And he whispered, "My friend," then ran off.

Lyndell didn't know if he meant her or the awful dog, but it gave her a warm feeling anyway.

The snow began that evening, lightly at first. Bennett shoved an old bench out near the dog so it could have some shelter, and the beast missed his leg by a full inch, out of appreciation. Muttering about the dog keeping away all the customers if the snow didn't, Benny sat down with his pipe.

Just in case anyone *did* venture out, Lyndell was prepared. Wearing the navy kerseymere—even more sacklike on her than Isabelle's grey—and the rest of her disguise, she stationed herself in the small private parlour where she could see the front entrance and hear what went on in the tap room. Dust cloth in hand, she was ready to save her country, if not her reputation. What she wasn't ready for, certainly, was Molly.

Coming into the parlour, snooping on *her*, most likely, Lyndell thought indignantly, Molly looked even more fallen by candlelight. She'd changed into a red satin-bodiced gown with lacings that didn't, or couldn't, do the job. Depending on the job, of course.

Lyndell had seen lightskirts before; one couldn't help but be aware of certain women in the park, or at the opera. Those were high fliers, though, elegant mistresses of the wealthy. She even knew some well-born widows, said to be "in keeping" as one would say "in mourning." Straw damsel, fancy piece, the muslin company, no euphemism quite fit the overripe Molly so well as "whore." But Molly was here, and Mrs. Bennett wasn't, so Lyndell could just stop being so old-maidish—perhaps her own dismal appearance was making her catty—and start snooping on her own.

"Do you think anyone will come out tonight?" she began. "It seems to be snowing harder."

"This is just the first of it. The ground's not froze up yet so it won't last. Some folks from the Manor'll stop by. Jake the groundskeeper'll see the lights. That's from King's Mark. D'you know him?"

Who was doing the questioning? Lyndell wondered. Of course she knew Jake, and of course he didn't know any Lynn Riddley. She improvised rapidly: "No, I don't know anyone in this area. I went to live with my mother's family when my father and Jasper came to King's Mark."

25

"Then you don't know Jasper too well, do you?" Molly asked, still probing.

"Well enough" was Lyndell's totally honest answer. "I haven't seen him recently, but we keep in touch with each other. That's why I'm here, of course."

"And did he happen to mention why he left so sudden like or when he'll be back?"

Lyndell couldn't tell whether she was being asked for answers, or just to test how much she knew. Molly had to know about the smuggling, and the dead courier at least, but she wasn't offering any information. Lyndell decided to give nothing away either. "He mentioned that he had a few problems and a few possibilities. Did he discuss anything with you?"

"No . . . He owes me some back wages, so I was just curious like."

It appeared to Lyndell that whatever else she knew, the other girl had no more knowledge of Jasper's whereabouts than his sister did. This was getting nowhere. Wiping industriously at a window pane, she casually enquired about the usual customers. "Besides the local working men and farmers, of course, I was wondering if any, well, titled gentlemen ever visited here."

Molly almost doubled over, laughing. "What, the country folk too rough for you? So you thought you'd throw your cap at some fine-breeched cove?" Still laughing, she made for the door and winked. "Let me tell you, dearie, no fancy gent's goin' t'offer the like o'you nobut a tupenny tumble, and that only if'n it's real dark."

The night wore on, tediously. It was Wednesday; she could be dancing at Almack's. A few locals clumped in, stomping the snow off their heavy boots in the hall. From her parlour she could hear them call for ale, joke with Molly. One or two even recognised Bennett, and many welcomed him back. From what Lyndell could hear of the conversations, none were anxious to talk of Jasper or the Quinns, most likely because of their own connexions with the smugglers. The talk centered on the snow: how long, how much, how bad for the crops and herds. Lyndell was yawning, considering going upstairs to bed. She didn't dare search Molly's room. Who knew how a lonely drover got ready for winter? And Jasper's belongings wouldn't offer much but dirt and debts. If he had any evidence of who was behind the smuggling or spying, he'd have given it to the authorities himself, to clear his name. On the other hand, he might more likely have used the proof to blackmail the traitor. Either way, he wouldn't have run. And where could he have run to?

Her thoughts were broken by a commotion outside: a carriage pulling up, the dog barking, carriage doors slamming, angry shouts, the sound of horses being whipped up and away. Lyndell stepped out of the parlour just as the front door crashed open. Cold air, a billow of snow, and a petite blond beauty holding a hatbox and wearing an ermine cape rushed in. The girl, sobbing hysterically, flew right into Lyndell's arms. Almack's was never like this!

Chapter Four

Lyndell pushed the newcomer through the parlour door and shut it on the gawking faces of the inn's customers as soon as she'd called for some hot tea. The girl was already standing by the fireside, holding her hands out to the warmth, still weeping. Lyndell helped remove the cape . . . and gasped. Under the fur, under exquisite gold ringlets only a trifle disordered, and enormous blue eyes just a bit reddened, and a magnificent collar of pearls too heavy for such a young, small girl, was the unmistakable black uniform and tiny white apron of a lady's maid.

"Good heavens, you've run away with your mistress's cape and jewellery!"

A watery giggle issued from the rosebud mouth. "It's the other way around, ma'am. I stole my maid's uniform, but the pearls are mine." Tears again. "And I am running away, but that awful man wouldn't take me to London after he took my money. He said it wasn't enough unless I ... I ... and the snow ... and now I don't even know where I am!"

Lyndell quickly handed over a handkerchief. "You're about an hour from Framingham, if that's a help, and I'm Miss Riddley. My brother owns this inn. Where did you ... run away from?"

"From Yorkshire, but I shan't go back, I would die first! Couldn't I stay here, please, ma'am? Only till I could earn enough for the coach to London? I'd work. I ... I could be your abigail?"

The dubious look that accompanied the question struck Lyndell's sense of humour. They both knew no self-respecting lady's maid would permit her employer to face the public rigged out the way Lyndell was. Her own Betty would have kittenfits at the very idea of the navy wool. Just in time to save Lyndell from having to explain her chuckle in the midst of such a dramatic plea, Sarah walked in with a tray.

"Ah, Mrs. Bennett, here is my maid from London, arrived at last." Lyndell spoke loudly, for the benefit of the tap room clientele.

Taking in the pearls, the cape, the kidskin half-boots—and the uniform—Sarah raised her eyebrows. Nobly, though, for the listeners, she replied, "And not a moment too soon."

Lyndell ignored the cryptic remark, directing Sarah to place the tea, then see to a fire in the room next to Lyndell's for her "maid." The instant the door was shut again she turned back to her teary visitor. She looked at the angelic face over the top rim of her uncle's spectacles—the only way she could see anything at all—and announced: "I'd be the first to admit that things are not always what they seem, and there are times when deceit becomes a necessity. This is not one of them, however. If you wish me to help you, you'll have to tell me the entire tale, with no roundaboutation, mind. No, I'm not going to toss you out in the snowy night like some unwashed baggage, you peagoose, so stop crying."

Perhaps it was the tea, or Lyndell's firm authority, or the reassuring "peagoose" she'd heard all her life, but the sniffling stopped and the story began.

Her name was Felicia Fullerton, she was seventeen, and, as Lyndell suspected, she was well born. Though the family was undistinguished, her parents were well connected and wealthy. Unsaid but implied was that they were also unable to cope with their headstrong, romantically inclined daughter. After hearing of the few "minor scrapes" this tiny beauty had landed in while still in the schoolroom, Lyndell could sympathise with them. The French tutor, the vicar's son, half of a naval installation—the chit had more hair than wits! Exasperated, the father decided to marry her off. . . .

"I just grew out of my braids and I'd have had to put on caps!" Miss Fullerton took one look at Lyndell's voluminous head-covering and began sobbing again, which didn't exactly help her cause. "No London season, no balls or parties!"

"Don't be silly, married ladies get presented too. They go to quite as many balls and with fewer restrictions. An arranged marriage mightn't be perfectly what you had in mind, but . . ."

But there was worse to come, she learned, between blubbers. Felicia's father had been in contact with an old friend, whose nephew was of an age to take a wife. Not only was the nephew *old*—at Lyndell's exclamation Felicia wisely added that thirty was too old for seventeen—but he was a retired soldier who'd been used to giving orders and being obeyed, just what her papa felt she needed.

"It . . . it might have been all right . . . some arranged marriages do work for the best. . . . I wouldn't mind being a marchioness, I think, and I would have tried to love my husband, and make him love me. But Cheyne is . . . is a Rake."

"Good Lord. The Marquis of Cheyne?"

"You see? Even you have heard of him."

For the past month or so, since the marquis had returned from the war in Belgium, Lyndell had heard of little else, though she'd never met him. He didn't attend Almack's, only the Cyprians' Ball. He wasn't seen at Sally Jersey's rout but he was spotted in Harriet Wilson's theatre box. He disdained the *Ton*, choosing instead the demi-mondaine, the other-world of gaming and fast women. *That* was the arranged *parti* for this innocent child? "Good heavens" was all Lyndell could think to say. .

"He'd never love me! He has his pick of every beautiful woman in London. They're sophisticated and . . . and smart. So you do see why I had to run away? He was coming to visit, his uncle wrote. I just had to leave."

Lyndell could see all too clearly: a loveless marriage to an unscrupulous libertine. She herself had been rejecting such offers for years. At least the marquis was known to be well-to-pass, so he wasn't after Felicia's money, unless he'd already gambled his considerable fortune away, but no, Felicia certainly would not be forced into this particular marriage. Lyndell would see to that!

Felicia giggled. "Well, I don't quite see what you can do, ma'am. I thought if I could just get to my aunt, Lady Forrester . . ."

"Lady Forrester has gone to Berkshire for her daughter's lying-in. You'll do better right here, you'll see."

Felicia nearly gaped. "Do you ... that is, could you ... know my aunt?" Felicia may have been a green country cloth-head, but she knew very well that her aunt did not number among her acquaintances dowdy ladies from hole-in-the-corner inns.

Lyndell did some long and hard thinking—an instant's flash of intuition, her best kind—and decided to reveal her own identity. "You'll recall that I mentioned things weren't always what they appeared. I'm not really Lynn Riddley, thank goodness; I'm tired of her already. My name is actually Lyndell Markham and, yes, I do know your aunt, and your cousin Elizabeth."

Laughing, Felicia said, "Miss Riddley, if you are the Magnificent Miss Markham, one of the most fashionable ladies in all London, I must be Princess Charlotte!"

Ruefully, Lyndell joined in the laughter. Then she removed the spectacles and the gruesome cap and shook out her curls. She wiped her face on a napkin while the younger girl watched, entranced. Finally Lyndell swept Miss Fullerton's ermine cape over her hideous navy sack and sank into her deepest court curtsey. "Your Majesty."

Later, In Lyndell's bedroom, the two young women made plans.

"You'll have to write to your father, saying you are visiting me at King's Mark. That will keep him from worrying, or searching. By the time he sends for you, the marquis should be long gone. If not, I'll take you into Berkshire myself. First we must catch a spy."

Felicia was suitably impressed and wide-eyed at Lyndell's tale of High Treason. Shivering delightedly at the warnings of danger, she clapped her hands when Lyndell assigned her the role of Felicity, lady's maid. She went off to her own room vowing this was the most thrilling thing that had ever happened in her whole life, and Miss Markham—Miss Riddley, that is—would never regret her new ally.

Lyndell, however, already did. She went to bed feeling remarkably old for twenty-four. Instead of having her own Grand Adventure, she felt more like the director of a play. A farce actually, even with the threat of violence. Her hero, Jasper, was a coward, her damsel in distress was a delightful widgeon. She had numerous disguises and false identities—and no clue as to the next scene.

Chapter Five

Mrs. Bennett brought Lyndell's chocolate early the next morning. She grumbled something about the "maid" being fast asleep, so Lyndell had to explain Felicia's predicament, and her decision to let the girl stay on.

"You'll see, it's working for the best. I've decided to visit Jasper's Captain Jamison this afternoon while Mr. Bennett goes to town. I'll make sure Benny has Miss Fullerton's letter to post, and a note for Tyler at King's Mark, in case anyone enquires for me. You have to remain here, naturally, so my maid Felicity is the perfect one to accompany me, the ever-so-respectable Miss Riddley." Her enthusiasm for Miss Riddley evaporated with the donning of the brown bombazine. Isabelle must have been four months increased when she had it fitted! "Did Joseph learn anything last night?" she asked, pinning her hair under the cap.

"He learned he's still good at draughts, nought

else. The local folks're wary of strangers, even if some knew us once. It takes time, Mr. Bennett says. Come now, Miss, the egg-man stopped by, so there's fresh for breakfast, and I've asked him to fetch us some chickens for dinner."

"Your chicken pie? Famous! Did the egg-man say how the roads were?"

"He said fair now, with the sun just out, but apt to turn mucky if it warms. Mr. Bennett says it feels like more snow in the air, in his finger joints likely, so you'd best get along with your errands for him."

When Lyndell reached the kitchen, Bennett was already out, "seeing about that cur with Sam'l." Lyndell hurried through her eggs and muffin, then made for the back door. Sarah stopped her with a smiling "It's right cold out—you'll need this."

"This" was an ancient and lumpy squirrel-lined wool shawl that must have done battle with moths— and lost. A relic of the departed Mrs. Quinn or left by a guest in lieu of payment, it undoubtably matched Lyndell's outfit far more suitably than her fur-lined green cloak.

"Complete to a shade, am I?" Lyndell asked, pirouetting across the kitchen. "But I shan't wear it when Felicity and I go to see Captain Jamison. He'd wonder that they had maids in the poorhouse!"

The dog's surroundings were improved by the bench for shelter, one of Sam'l's blankets for warmth and a bowl for fresh water. Its temper, if anything, was worse.

Bennett and Sam'l stood out of range, tossing small chunks of meat. Whenever they took a step closer, however, the huge brown beast charged, snapping.

"Here, let me try," offered Lyndell, but Bennett would have none of that.

"Oh, no, miss. The dog's mean. Most likely been whipped so often it won't let anyone near. See the marks on's back?"

"How terrible! No wonder the poor thing is mean. But Sam'l, I thought he was your friend. Won't he let you touch him either?"

Sam'l just looked down, so Bennett answered for him: "Likely Quinn whipped the boy too, so he feels sorry for the beast." The small figure in his cut-down jacket just shivered.

Lyndell felt her throat close up. She wouldn't cry though; that would help nothing. Instead, she firmly declared, "Well, no one shall hurt either of them again, ever. Give me the bowl. If it was Quinn who hurt the dog, maybe your voice and the smell of horses remind him. . . . Here Ajax, nice dog; good dog Ajax," she called softly, crooning as she slowly inched forward, tossing small bites of food until she was almost close enough to offer a bit in her fingers. Her method seemed to be working, for Ajax made no effort to charge at her, and he'd stopped making the gnarring sound deep in his throat between swallows. Very gingerly Lyndell held her hand out and just as fearfully Ajax accepted the morsel. Another step. Maybe he'd sniff her hand or let her pet him? At the last step what she saw made her gasp and jerk her arm back. Her sudden movement caused Ajax to go stiff-legged and snarly and *his* return to hostility made Lyndell back away. Very slowly.

"It's awful!" She told Bennett when she reached his side. She barely noticed that he put down a sturdy log he'd been holding. "The dog's neck is all raw and the rope is cutting right into it! He must be vicious with the pain! Who could do a thing like that?"

"They must have tied him as a pup, then he got too mean to handle so they just left him. Happens that way. Couldna' been too long. He's not full growed, for all his size."

"Well, we'll just have to cut it off him." A knife appeared from under Bennett's leather smock. "Right. *I'll* have to cut it off him." This time she waited to make sure Bennett had a firm grip on the log before approaching Ajax.

Maybe the poor brute saw a man with a weapon; maybe he'd just had enough to eat. Either way, he wasn't letting Lyndell get near him.

"Good Ajax. I know someone hurt you, poor doggie," she chanted, approaching step by slow step. Ajax retreated, growling low. Lyndell put the bowl of food down, thinking that she would work on the rope collar while Ajax lowered his head to eat, but the dog didn't lower his head. Just as she reached her hand out again, saying "we're only trying to help you," the dog lunged and snapped his jaws shut a hair's breadth from her fingers.

"I don't think he understood about our helping," Lyndell gasped, again next to Bennett, handing back the knife. "What do we do now? If we untie the chain, he'll just run away and die. If we leave him . . ."

"He'll die. Infection or chokin' or starvin' when he can't swallow no more. It'd be kinder to end his sufferin' right now. I'm sorry, laddie," he told Sam'l, "but you can't want him to go on hurtin' so bad, now can you?"

Lyndell couldn't see the boy's face, his chin tucked so tight against his collar, but she saw his head shake, then a tear fell on his scuffed and ragged boot-top. What about the boy's suffering?

"Not yet, Benny. We can give it a few more days, can't we? He's not sickly and he's eating fine and—you saw—he almost let me pet him. I can keep trying, bringing him treats, talking to him. Maybe he'll let me work on the rope tomorrow, or the next day. What do you say?"

"I say you never listened to me about tryin' to fix a busted sparrow neither." He pulled a handkerchief from his pocket and turned away to blow his nose.

Lyndell was finding it a little hard to swallow herself. She cleared her throat before telling Bennett and Sam'l she had to see about writing a letter for the butler at King's Mark.

Chapter Six

$\mathcal{L}$yndell was driving Jasper's curricle, wearing her green cloak. "Felicity" was sitting beside her, wearing the decrepit squirrel shawl and a frown. She couldn't quite see why, if she couldn't wear her ermine cape because a maid *wouldn't*, she couldn't flirt with the egg-man, which a maid would. Lyndell was dizzy from trying to explain how pretending to be a serving girl had nothing to do with acting like a lady. She almost thought she was doing the Marquis of Cheyne a favour.

For now she had to push Felicity's problems to the back of her mind. There was the dog, and there was Jasper—*where* was Jasper?—Molly, and this Captain Drew Jamison at the Southwold Barracks, the one who was investigating the murdered courier. How much of Jasper's letter could she reveal? For that matter, how unentangled was Jasper in the whole affair? On reflection, she realised that she had only his word that he knew nothing of

Quinn's doings, and Jasper's word was something less solid than Stonehenge. So what was she doing here, driving the sorriest nags she'd even been behind—trust Jasper to own retired plowhorses—over slush-covered roads that she couldn't even see? She snatched the benighted spectacles off her nose and threw them into Felicia's lap.

"Take these," she said, "and remind me to put them on when we arrive."

The reminder of Lyndell's own sacrifices seemed to moderate Felicia's indignation. She brightened up, under the dreadful grey shawl, and began questioning her dear Lyndy about "the Season." If Lyndell had ever been that eager she certainly couldn't recall it. Of course, she'd never been as sheltered as Miss Fullerton; she had attended small parties well before she was officially "out," becoming accustomed to Society from her earliest days. Maybe that was why she was so . . . well, jaded was the word she thought of, so bored with Society. Maybe she should retire to Suffolk permanently, and grow roses (which made her sneeze). Maybe she should just reconsider Isabelle's advice about a comfortable hus—

"Halt, who goes there?"

Captain Jamison took thirty minutes to decide to see Miss Lynn Riddley. During this time she sat in the carriage, chilled, impatiently tapping her foot on the floorboard, while Felicity/Felicia smiled at every passing soldier, and every soldier in the whole fort found a reason to inspect the carriage and its dainty occupant. Felicity was adorable, despite the shawl, which she managed to slip off her shoulders, baring enough to the chill air to raise goosebumps on the pink flesh. The black of her uniform, crisply pressed again, hemmed and gathered by Mrs. Bennett to mould the plumply rounded figure, well became the girl's rosy colouring. The blond curls, which neither Lyndell nor Felicia had been able to manage creditably, were gathered up onto Felicia's head with a scrap of black lace ribbon from one of Lyndell's petticoats, letting the ringlets fall down her back. Not quite right for a lady's maid, but extremely pleasing to a handsome young corporal begging to know where such a lovely flower had sprung from. Lyndell had the dreadful thought that Felicia might mention the King's Pass Inn by name, filling the tavern with panting soldiers. Lyndell's vivid imagination could see Bennett beating them off with his log while Molly got rich. Not a moment too soon, Lyndell kicked her companion soundly on the ankle, causing that young lady to blush and finally lower those blue eyes. Miss Riddley, at her own haggish worst, froze the soldier with a daunting grimace through the distorting lenses.

Then a young private, a boy really, stammered to Felicia that the captain could see her mistress now. The rush to hand Felicia down could have routed the French years earlier; Miss Riddley had to accept the reluctant hand of what looked like the company cook. At least his stained apron suggested that, though why he'd be standing near the gate was beyond her. If this was how the army was run, no wonder secrets could be stolen . . . unless caution was much relaxed now that the war was finally over and these men would soon be civilians. No matter. She firmly gripped Felicia's upper arm and pulled the girl along with her after the private.

Captain Jamison greeted them in an anteroom, buttoning his uniform jacket, with effort, over a low paunch. His eyes gave Miss Riddley the merest glance at the introduction, straying to Felicity for a thorough look. While he was thus discourteously occupied, Lyndell conducted her own investigation, over the spectacles' rims.

Jamison was fortyish, one of those gentlemen who try to act younger and succeed in seeming older, or foolish. He had thin blond hair of a wishy-washy colour, combed into a wish-he-had-more style, streaky bands pulled across his head and spread out to cover more territory. His eyes, travelling up and down Felicity's charming figure, were damp-ish, with disappearing white lashes. There were crumbs in his yellow moustache. Altogether Captain Jamison was not Lyndell's ideal picture of an English officer.

When she explained that her mission was of a private, delicate nature, he gruffly gestured her to the inner office. Lyndell pushed Felicity into one of the outer chamber's two chairs and whispered as forcefully as she could, "Sit there and *do* be quiet." She gave a last vicious look to the young private, who reddened and then fled outside, before she followed Jamison, shutting the door behind her.

Jamison was already at his desk, lighting a cigar with brown-stained fingers. He impatiently waved the foul item in the vague direction of a chair, then sat down. If she'd come as Miss Lyndell Markham, she thought, this pompous little twit would be hopping up and down, offering her wine or tea or the best seat and hanging on her every word. There was a lesson to be learned there, Lyndell realised, one she would have to consider seriously at a later point, a moral she knew would be good for her soul. Right now, however, the lesson she was learning— had learned quite well already—was that she en-joyed being Lyndell Markham far more than she did being Miss Lynn Riddley! This afternoon, however, she had to be plain—Lyndell chuckled to herself at that double-edged word—Miss Riddley, with no authority and no right to demand courtesy. She was simply Jasper's spinster sister, come to see if she could help clear her brother's name.

"No, no, ma'am, there's nothing you can do . . . unless of course you know where Riddley might be right now. My superiors were not pleased with his disappearing."

"Is . . . is he suspected of anything?"

"There's no certain proof. They merely want to talk to him."

"His nerves were so overset by this whole situation, he had to take a repairing lease. His health, you know, has always been delicate."

The captain picked at his fingernails with a penknife. "No, I didn't. Frankly, ma'am, I don't see what you're doing here. If Riddley has nothing to hide, he should be out in the open. If not, he's well out of it. So why don't you just go on back to where you come from and let us handle it."

Of all the patronising pap! He may as well be patting her on the head, while fitting Jasper for a hemp necktie! "Sir, I feel I'd do better at the inn waiting for the London gentleman Jasper mentioned as having some connexion with the messenger who was murdered."

Jamison gave her a hard look. "A London gentleman, eh? He didn't speak of it to me before he loped off. What else did he happen to mention?"

"Why . . . why nothing else. Just that a murder was committed, secret documents were involved, and you were questioning him. That must mean you suspected the inn was involved. But it was the Quinns who ran off—"

"Aye, the Quinns. Let me tell you, Miss Riddley, the Quinns may have had more to hide than your brother. Maybe not. But Mrs. Quinn was found drowned up near Yarmouth this week. Maybe in a scuttled smuggler's boat trying to escape to France, and just maybe made to look like a drowning by someone who didn't want her talking." He held up three fingers of one hand, fingernails still dirty, Lyndell noted, even in her horror. "Maybe that someone was Quinn"—he bent down the first finger. "Maybe your London gentleman." The second. "And maybe your precious brother Jasper."

She gasped, but he went on, brutally: "I'm not saying what I suspect, but I am saying it's no place for you. Traitors don't sit around drinking tea, ma'am, and reading sermons. And murderers, two-time murderers, don't care much for manners! So go do your good works, lady, somewhere else." His voice had raised to a bellow at the end, but Lyndell did not flinch.

"Jasper is not a spy. Nor is he a murderer." She stood in quiet determination. In some belated regard for the amenities, Jamison stood also. His efforts at placating her having failed, and his attempt to frighten her away as well, he gave up in exasperation. "Very well, go back to your flea-ridden inn and wait for your Town nob. Send me a message if you find any proof."

"Thank you, Captain, I'll certainly do that."

She extricated Felicia from a knot of soldiers—someone had offered *her* tea—and stalked out to the waiting carriage. The captain handed her up, then Felicia, who turned to wave gaily back at her new admirer.

"Abominable girl! Don't encourage them. Especially not that despicable Captain Drew Jamison."

"Isn't he though? He even pinched me on the way out."

Despite all the turmoil raging in her head, Lyndell still had an ounce of pity to spare for any man unfortunate enough to marry this brazen chit. She snapped the reins to get her team to a steady gait, one just possibly faster than she could walk, and removed the eyeglasses as soon as the Southwold gates were behind her.

Even before Miss Riddley had her back to him, Captain Jamison stomped to his office, shouted for a messenger, stubbed out his cheroot and scrawled a note:

"Jasper Riddley's sister here, asking about London gent. Advise."

Chapter Seven

$\mathcal{L}$yndell was depressed. Things were going from horrid to hellish. She could have done Jasper as much good by staying in London! And then she wouldn't have involved her dear friends the Bennetts in this maelstrom. Nor would she have encouraged Felicia to stay where the girl's very life might be threatened. As for the boy and the dog and this wretched inn, how in the world did she get to be responsible for all of them?

She'd returned from the visit to Jamison at another cloud-early dusk, to a scene of perfect tranquillity. Bennett and Sam'l were counting harness, the boy nodding as Benny slowly and clearly gave each a number. Mrs. Bennett was at the kitchen table, her pots bubbling on the stove, stitching new curtains from the fabric Joseph had fetched back from Entwood, the nearest town. Tiny red roses on a cream background. Another murder, and Sarah was sewing curtains! She already knew about the murder, it seemed, gossip in Entwood being full of that. No one had actually blamed Jasper, Bennett had reported, but everyone was wondering where he was, that was certain!

"Tongues running on wheels, I'd wager. But why shouldn't I be making new hangings? It's no great expense, and'll make the place ever so much more homey. If we decide to leave, why, the new people will have a friendlier welcome. And as for the boy, he'll need to count just as well in Islington, now won't he?" Sarah looked so content, so sure the world was a good place for her and hers, Lyndell hadn't the heart to argue.

She took a bowl of chicken scraps set aside for the dog, and tried that futile task once more. Ajax let her approach, and even licked her fingers. But when she attempted to bring the knife toward his neck, he lurched away. He didn't try to snap at her and wasn't growling so loudly; he would not let her touch him, however. She was hesitant about trying again, not for fear of being bitten anymore so much as of injuring the dog worse with the sharp knife if he continued the sudden moves. He ate the chicken, but he held his head to one side, stiffly.

Sam'l was watching her face intently for a sign of hope, and she had none to give him. She placed a dry blanket under the dog's bench.

Dinner was a dismal affair, despite Sarah's chicken pies. Lyndell had tried to convince Felicia to return home. It was just too dangerous here, she told the girl, without, for Sam'l's sake, mentioning the fate of Mrs. Quinn. There was a world of difference between a genteel spy, she warned, no matter how treacherous, and a hardened killer. Bennett could go into Entwood and hire a carriage and driver, trustworthy ones, so Felicia would be safe.

47

The girl would have none of it, especially now that things were getting exciting. No, she wouldn't go to her aunt in Berkshire, to Lyndell's aunt in London, not even to stay at King's Mark. No threats of possible scandals could shake her determination to remain. Besides, Lyndell needed her. Hadn't she been handy this day? Wasn't she to stand guard while Lyndell searched Molly's room? When the cornflower blue eyes started to fill with tears, Lyndell relented, against her better judgement. Felicia instantly decided to be a proper maid and bounced up to serve the coffee, spilling some, of course. The stain wouldn't be too visible on the brown bombazine. That was the bright side.

Bennett had nothing more to report from his visit to the village. And no one at King's Mark seemed to know about Jasper, "though old Tyler's getting past it, Miss. I expect you could hide the Prince Regent and his cronies in that great barracks of a place 'n Tyler'd not notice." Bennett would have to make a less overt visit sometime, to get a better look. He'd given Tyler Miss Markham's note, saying she was on her way, but if anyone asked, she was simply not receiving. Bennett didn't hold much confidence in the old man's understanding, though, so if any London acquaintances should stop by, by chance or Aunt Hardesty's direction, they might be told she hadn't yet arrived! What a furor that would cause! Another thing to worry about; a worry she scarcely needed.

The search of Molly's room, while she was safely at her own supper, prolonged by Bennett's conversation, was another wasted effort. Lyndell learned a great deal about a tart's tastes (garish) and habits (sloppy), but nothing about spies. Unlike Jasper, Molly didn't seem to accumulate possessions, just a hoard of paste jewellery and tawdry bonnets with wax cherries. Even the false cherries had chips in them.

Jasper's rooms were being made neater, in stages. Felicia was delighted with this task, learning more about a gentleman's habits than she'd learned in her short lifetime. Or than was good for her, according to Mrs. Bennett. Lyndell had to agree, but it was either keep the chit busy with Jasper's discards, or listen to her pleas to go downstairs to serve the customers!

The only evidence that Jasper was guilty of anything but decadence was a nearly empty bottle of fine brandy—obviously French. Obviously smuggled. The inch remaining must have been an oversight, which Lyndell decided to correct once she was alone in her bedchamber. It was the least she could do.

It took Lyndell's coach six or seven hours to reach East Entwood from London, making a few stops. A neck-or-nothing rider on army business, changing horses often, could make the round trip in just over ten hours. So it was that at two-thirty that Friday morning, when Lyndell was fast asleep, having disposed of the evidence, Captain Jamison received the reply to his message:

"Jasper Riddley has no sister. Tell Quinn to get rid of the woman."

Chapter Eight

It may have been a cold, stormy day in November, but the fates were playing Maygames with Lyndell's future. There she was, safe and warm in her bed, for the present, while in London at that same fatal hour, Wesley Richardson, Marquis of Cheyne, was living up to his reputation.

Not his reputation as a war hero, though that was considerable, Cheyne having served as a much decorated aide under Wellesley and often been mentioned in the despatches. Nor his reputation as a lady's man, if ladies they could be called, which he'd been earning this past month since his return, as if there were no women in Spain, Portugal or Belgium. No, it was his reputation for disdaining the polite world, for pursuing his own pleasures— and conventions be damned. In other words, my lord marquis was in his shirt-sleeves, in a low dive, dicing and drunk. His companions around the baize table were as jug-bitten as he, young members of the idle upper class, using Cheyne's return from the wars as a good enough reason to celebrate.

If any chance observer was asked to pick the ex-soldier from the bunch, his unerring choice would be Cheyne. Not the tallest nor the broadest, he was still the most substantial looking, the most well-muscled of these gentlemen, although they were all Corinthians, sportsmen who worked out at Jackson's boxing parlour, Manton's shooting gallery and Antoine's fencing school. His skin, darkened by seven years of rough outdoor living, contrasted with his companions' fashionable city pallor. His face, also, while certainly handsome with its square jaw and sculptured lines, was more lined as if, at thirty, he had lived longer and harder than his associates, mostly his cousin Willy's cronies. Not all the lines were from polite laughter; there were scars of bitterness from a war that was not all political debate and military tactics. Call it an air of weariness mixed with that of strength and confidence; he was easy to spot.

What was hard for some to understand was why this member of the nobility was not attending Princess Lieven's rout, not being lionised at the Prince Regent's salon, not being fawned over by every matron and macaroni in the *Ton*. The solution was simple: Cheyne did not trust himself in polite society. When he'd first returned, there were the unavoidable family homecoming dinners, the obligatory royal receptions. The men all wanted to congratulate him on the smashing victory at Quatre Bras—later to be know as Waterloo—and the ladies wished to gossip about the Duchess of Richmond's battle-eve ball . . . at which all the young lads had their last dance, their last stolen kisses, before marching off to war, some still in their satin breeches and silk stockings, to be found days later, their bodies rotting on muddy fields. Hundreds upon hundreds, and only the lucky had died quickly. The horses were more fortunate—details were sent out to despatch the wounded and dying, to stop the awful screaming.

. . . Heroic victory, scintillating ball . . . the worst nightmare that Wesley, Lord Cheyne had ever seen, would ever see, for all his days on earth. No, he'd go no more to listen to the chitchat, to smile while his gut wrenched, to dance with all the pretty little girls who wanted to know the man of the hour. Here, in Willy's and his friends' company, Cheyne could forget it all, even if it took a bottle of Blue Ruin to do it. And these men would not bother him for battle facts, not these grown boys who'd stayed home. Some were embarrassed that they hadn't done their duty, while others envied him the chance to go. They all respected him . . . and everyone but his own cousin feared him.

It was Willy, William Richardson, Baronet, who teased him, who chivvied him with swaggering bravado, to bring the laughter back to those tired eyes. And it was Willy, best loved and almost-brother, who still resented not being able to join up when his hero Wes, at twenty-three five years Willy's senior, went off to war.

Willy's father had still had two years of control over his nephew before Cheyne came into his full inheritance, and Viscount Richardson was bound and determined to keep his cherished nephew out of danger as long as he could. The young marquis, even then strong-willed and steady of purpose, was just as resolute about buying colours and fighting for his country. It took him a long time to convince his Uncle George, but he succeeded, after getting up to every rig and row in Town—and letting Willy tag after him. There'd been duels and demi-reps, nights when poor Uncle George had to stand bail for both his wayward charges, and days when he had to listen to his wife's weeping.

When it came to Cheyne, the viscount bowed to the inevitable, but not for Willy. Oh no, Willy was too young, Willy was the heir, not just to his father's considerable estates but to Cheyne's vaster holdings and titles. Willy had to finish school. Willy had to console his mother for her dear nephew's absence, after she'd raised the boy from childhood to be her other son. So every time in the seven years of his service that Cheyne returned on leave, or to be reassigned, or was sent to plead before Parliament for more funds for the struggling armies, Willy tried his best to prod his cousin to battle. He wanted the chance to whip old Wes at fisticuffs, to outshoot him, outride, or outdrink him, even outargue him. Sometimes he even managed to do it, too, which made Willy feel a lot better about things in general. It was that kind of night. For his part Cheyne seemed to sympathise with Willy's need to prove himself. He enjoyed crossing wits or swords with his cousin, and just as cheerfully lost as won, cementing a friendship begun when Willy was still gurgling in his cradle.

Occasionally Cheyne had even been known to goad the quick-tempered Willy, just out of a quirky humour. It was that kind of night, too.

"No, bantling, I still say there's no such thing as an honest woman; they're all selling something. Take a whore, now"—ribald laughter from the company—"she at least sets a price and gives fair value." The marquis smiled at his companions, a

53

lopsided grin that took years off his age. "But your so-called virtuous woman—hah! She's only holding out for higher stakes! A man's name, his title, his money, his home. And what does he get? Some sweet young thing to warm his bed at night? To see to his comfort? No, he gets a headachy shrew or a watering pot 'doing her duty'!"

Willy was no more in the petticoat line than the other young men present, yet just to contradict his cousin, he felt he must defend the fairer sex. After all, his mother was a woman, and his sister. "Beg to differ with you, Wes, but you've been out of the country too long. Maybe your señoritas and mademoiselles can't be trusted, but English girls—"

"Englishwomen? They're the worst! They're bred to be warmblooded mistresses or coldhearted ladies, and they've never understood the two could mix. Not that you'd want to marry your mistress, but damn, these 'ladies' your mother trots out for me every time I'm home are like ice maidens!"

While Willy was thinking of a rebuttal, even his wine-fogged head saw the trap: he was going to be forced to defend the institution of marriage itself. The next thing he knew, *he'd* be getting leg-shackled instead of Wesley. He'd known his cousin too long.

Then Ferddie Milbrooke, notoriously mild-mannered, tried to change the subject. "But what of affection, Cheyne? Haven't you ever been in love?"

The marquis tossed the dice in the air. "Love? Why yes, I've been in love," he drawled. "Sometimes thrice a night."

At the other men's laughter, Willy reentered the discussion. "And what of the lady you'll marry someday? Shan't you love her?" he asked curiously.

"If you are thinking of the little northern heiress your father's picked out for me, there's a greater chance I'll grow wings and fly to Yorkshire. Those country girls are the worst of all, rigid morality and no social graces to compensate. No, halfling, just because I'll put a ring on some girl's finger doesn't mean she'll put one through my nose."

Willy *had* in fact been thinking of Miss Felicia Fullerton, a girl he'd known for years. He recalled a tiny china doll—certainly not some cloddish milk-maid—and it didn't suit his new-found ideas of pro-priety for Wesley to be bantering about his intended like this. With inebriated belligerence, Willy de-manded, "Then why in blazes are you going there?"

"Why, to look over the merchandise, of course."

Now, the real reason the Marquis of Cheyne had acquiesced to his uncle's wishes, after listening to innumerable lectures on his duties and responsibil-ities, how he owed it to the ancient and honourable name to settle down, etc., was because the trip to Yorkshire fit his plans. There was a bit of business the War Office wanted him to look into, some loose ends to tidy up, and here was the perfect alibi for leaving town. He had no intention of offering for the girl, of course. He'd see to his errand, then he'd politely suggest to Miss Fullerton's father that she should know more of the world before making a choice, then he would excuse himself. As he ex-plained to his Uncle George, perhaps he was ready for a little peace and comfort, learning to manage his estates and be a country gentleman. But not with a seventeen-year-old schoolgirl bride! He had nothing against Miss Fullerton, of course—he'd never even heard of the chit before—and he actu-ally had nothing against marriage—for the right fellows!—and women he thoroughly enjoyed. No, his words were mostly the result of the wine and his desire to rile poor Willy. They had the intended effect, of course.

"To look over the merchandise, you cad! To speak of Miss Fullerton like that is insulting and degrading. I won't have it, do you hear?"

"But my dear William, I'm sure I never mentioned Miss Fullerton by name. You did! And if she's my intended, or shall we say intended-to-be-seen, I don't see what you can do about it."

"Well . . . well," Lord Richardson sputtered, "she's to be the head of my household, so I have the right to defend her honour! And I will and I do! You'll meet me for this!"

As the other men laughed, Cheyne called for another bottle. "But of course, cuz, I always do! What's it to be this time? Pistols or swords?"

Willy was laughing now too. "Come, Wes, you have the choice, I challenged you, remember?"

"So you did. Well, my poor battered face don't need another scar, and I'm too foxed for swords, so let's try pistols. They're quicker anyway."

Chapter Nine

$\mathcal{T}$here were rigid codes for *Affaires of Honour*. Seconds for both sides would meet and discuss conditions and select a secluded location. A surgeon was hired for the injured; a carriage often stood waiting to whisk the victor out of the country in case his man stuck his spoon in the wall. Being illegal, duels were secretive, hushed affairs. All parties would gather at dawn in formal dress, the seconds would make a last *pro forma* effort at conciliation, the weapons would be inspected, the ground marked out. . . .

In the trash-heaped, snow-blotted back yard of the Goose and Garter Tavern, Sir Fenton Crestwicke was making bets with a pickpocket and a rag merchant while the attics-to-let Richardson cousins staggered outside, holding each other up and singing the fifth chorus of "The Mermaid from Dover." So much for *Affaires of Honour*. The Marquis of Queensbury be damned. All of Willy and Cheyne's friends, all more than slightly on the go, were having a delightful time, laying odds, clearing a space of rubbish, setting out torches in the snow. It was just another exhibition of skill as far as they were concerned, by two of the best shots in England. Usually the Richardsons shot each other's hats off, though once Cheyne had managed to pop Willy's new beaver while aiming upside down and backwards between his own legs. That was the stunt which finally got him his army commission. That was also why Wesley and his cousin now simply struck while the iron was hot, as it were, before Uncle George got wind of anything, before Aunt Wilhelmina could develop palpitations.

The pistols were primed. It was to be seven paces, turn and shoot, no dropped handkerchiefs or "Gentlemen, take aim." Back to back, Cheyne, the taller by some inches, told his cousin, "Loser buys breakfast," and Willy answered, "As always." As they took the first step, however, Cheyne was telling himself that maybe he really *should* think of settling down and stopping such tomfoolery. So at the third step he called "Hold." He bent down, as though to remove an obstacle or adjust a bootstrap. It was hard to tell, in the shadows, and Cheyne's greatcoat hid his actions from Willy and the observers. In a moment he straightened, said "Sorry. Let's continue." Four steps . . . . five, six and seven.

Cheyne turned, raised his right arm, and fired— a snowball, which hit Willy smack in the face!

"Wesley Richardson, you blackhearted shabster! Of all the low-minded—" Willy squawked, his friends hooting. Then Willy bent low, dropping the pistol in order to gather his own like weapon for counterattack. A primed and loaded dueling pistol, however, is not the type of inanimate object that can be so casually treated, which the young baronet would have recalled if he weren't so castaway, or so anxious for revenge.

The pistol exploded, the noise echoing off the buildings facing the lot, deafening in the sudden silence.

"By all that's holy, Wes, I think I've shot m'toes off!"

It could have been worse, Cheyne realised. Hell, a dropped pistol could have taken the fool's head off. Instantly cold sober, Cheyne had found himself shaking. So many friends lost, and now this most precious of all almost killed without even the pitiful excuse of a war. Never again, he vowed. As they got Willy back to their shared lodgings where Farrow, Cheyne's ex-batman, was competently slicing Willy's boot off, Cheyne kept repeating, "no more chances." His uncle was right, they were too old, they had to settle down. Life was suddenly much too valuable. When Farrow declared that Willy's foot was one bloody mess, but not like to be serious at all, barring fever or infection, the marquis made his decision: Willy'd go with him to Yorkshire. He couldn't be left to face the viscount's lectures alone—even Cheyne wasn't that hardhearted—nor to have Lady Richardson fuss over him. No, first they'd make excuses to the family, then travel to Suffolk where Willy could recuperate and Cheyne would take care of his errand. Then it was on to Yorkshire: settling down, matrimony, securing the succession and all that—for Willy. Cheyne vowed to see his cousin safely settled and out of harm's way by the new year. Naturally, he didn't tell Willy. Handing him a glass of port while Farrow sprinkled basilicum powder over the now-cleaned foot before bandaging it, Cheyne told his cousin to drink up.

"We've got to appear thoroughly foxed if we're not to make mice feet of getting by the governor."

Willy would have fallen right off the couch, laughing so hard, if Farrow hadn't held on to his foot. "Damne, Wes, if I weren't thoroughly foxed now, do'you think I'd be here like this?"

The two cousins staggered up the front steps of Richardson House, Grosvenor Square, holding each other up, singing the sixth chorus of "The Mermaid from Dover," very loudly. Since it was now four o'clock in the morning, it was very loud indeed. They let themselves in with Willy's key, and stood in the entranceway, arms around each other, beginning the seventh verse. The eighth verse did it. Doors opened up and down halls, servants came running. But it was the governor himself, Viscount Richardson, in his nightcap, who outdid his son and nephew in volume.

"This is the finish! I've had my fill of the two of you! I'll disinherit you both, see if I don't! Get out! Get out and don't let me see your faces till you've learned some respect. Do you hear me?"

There must have been no one in Grosvenor Square who didn't hear him. Willy grinned and nodded foolishly, but Cheyne, worried for his uncle's health—the viscount was turning red and quivering with indignant rage—was politely reassuring. "Yes, shir. We jusht came to say g'bye—off to Yorkshire, don't ya know, to get reshpectable. Takin' Willy for courage. . . . He's always been up in the boughs when I didn't take him before, don'tcha know."

"Yes, yes, get out! 'Tho I wouldn't let a daughter

of mine marry either one of you! Now go before the whole household is awakened."

Even the dead, of course, were nearly wakened, so loud was the prior discussion, but it sufficed. The door was almost slammed in their faces and Farrow and Cheyne could half drag, half carry Willy to the coach. Farrow bundled him in with fur rugs and hot bricks, amid the hurriedly packed bags, while Cheyne checked the horses tied behind. When the marquis walked around to the front to take the ribbons, Willy leaned out of the still open door.

"Say, Wes, are we really going to Yorkshire?"

"Yes, you clunch, and maybe you'll be sober by the time we get there!"

Chapter Ten

$\mathcal{F}$riday morning was grey: grey overcast sky, Isabelle's grey good-works dress, grey face powder over her own peach complexion, a grey, grey mood. Miss Markham was so rarely out of sorts that she had no patience now for her own ill humour. Surely she wasn't missing the empty-headed frivolities of Town, nor the adulation of her prosy admirers. She couldn't be that shallow. Nor would she own that her Great Adventure was turned into a tedious, frustrating interval. No, it must be the weather that had her in the mopes, and she chided herself. The sun was sure to come out sooner or later, and something just had to relieve this idle waiting. If not, she decided, in a few days she'd move the whole ménage, except Molly, up to King's Mark, resume her own identity, perhaps even invite some guests for a country visit. Bennett could keep an eye on the inn, and Jasper could pull his own coals out of the fire. That's what she'd do—in a few days. This morning after breakfast, however, she'd tackle Jasper's accounts, what smidgens of bookkeeping she could find, to see if they told her anything. Just having a constructive course of action cheered her spirits. Something was bound to happen.

Mrs. Bennett was singing to her fresh dough, encouraging the loaves to rise. Obviously there were no clouds on *her* horizon, except Molly, of course. There would be girls from the village coming to help clean this morning, some apples she'd found put up to make into pies. Her man was content gossiping with the tradesfolk and farmers, though he mentioned having to obtain better horses, if they stayed. And the boy had mumbled the whisperiest—and sweetest—"Thank you" she'd ever heard, just for some slab bacon and eggs. If only Miss Lyndy would forget her notions about smugglers and spies, take the pretty little miss with her back to London so Mrs. Bennett didn't have to worry over them, then everything would be just perfect. Except Molly.

"That . . . the trollop must go, Miss Lyndy! Why, last night she pinched Mr. Bennett's cheek!"

"Sarah, I think you're jealous!"

Although the older woman's face reddened, she denied it with vigour. "Fustian! At his age? But it isn't right, what with that sweet Miss Felicity to see such havey-cavey carryings-on."

Lyndell was spreading jam on a bun. She paused to lick her fingers before reassuring Mrs. Bennett. "I misdoubt Molly could teach Felicia anything! That girl could smile at a grandfather clock and have it skip an hour! Molly has to stay a while longer, you know, in case our London beau ever arrives. So we can tell if she knows him or not. Don't worry, pet, it can't be long now, something's bound to happen!"

Another futile session with Ajax—he was weakening, but not in his distrust—forced her to admit that time was shortening there too, without much to show. Her only hope was that by the next day he'd be too sick to struggle.

Jasper's books, what there were of them, were more enlightening than Lyndell had expected. Sitting at Jasper's desk, trying to decipher his crabbed hand, she first attacked the ledger, and discovered why any gentlemen ever came to such a backwater inn. In amongst "J. Anthony, locksmith" and "T. Phutts, merchant" were interspersed entries like "Lord F. and Lady T. . . . Sir J. and Miss L.R. . . . Lord H-M. and companion." All those couples . . . all those unmarried couples! Jasper was allowing the inn to be used as a trysting place! Goodness, let them try it with Mrs. Bennett in charge! Lyndell chuckled, until she realised what a great opportunity this gave the spy to be where he shouldn't. No one would think it remarkable if just another London swell was at King's Pass, waiting for his "companion" to arrive.

Turning to the accounts books, scraps of tradesmen's bills stuffed in envelopes, Lyndell made another observation: while there were the usual expenses for salaries and supplies, these were mostly for foodstuffs, fuel, ale, and horse feeds. Nowhere was there a bill or a receipt for wine, or brandy, or port, not even a note from a whiskey distributor. Yet Lyndell had seen the well-stocked shelves, the nearly full wine cellar. She'd even partaken of some herself. The only conclusion possible, she acknowledged sadly, was that Jasper simply wasn't paying for those bottles. If he wasn't paying in cash, he must be trading—what? Silence? A place for the free-booters to store their loads as they brought the stuff inland? Use of his horses and wagon? There was no way of knowing the degree of Jasper's involvement, but it must be considerable. So what should she do now? Go to the authorities? He was still her step-brother. Burn the evidence? The bottles would still be there without their customs stamps. No, what she had to do was find Jasper, and get him out of the country once and for all! If it took threatening him with his own account books, she'd do it! In the meantime, Lyndell stashed the records in her valise. If the authorities chose to search Jasper's rooms, there was no need to make things easier for them, and if they happened to find them in his sister's closet, no matter. She was studying them—to learn the business.

One part of the business the accounts didn't teach had to do with salaries. The Quinns drew theirs monthly, the inn's maidservants were paid weekly, occasional village help, daily. Sam'l was paid twice, a shilling each time, with expenses for his boots and pants marked in. The curious part was Molly, not mentioned anywhere that Lyndell could find. That afternoon, passing the common room on her way to the front parlour, Lyndell thought to ask the girl about it.

"It's a trade of course, my room 'n keep in exchange for waitin' on tables. And what the gentlemen give me I get to keep for myself. A girl's got to get along, you know." She snickered, bringing an urge to do mischief to Lyndell's usually well-controlled temper. "Or maybe you don't."

Lyndell fled to the parlour before her urge to throw something got the better of her. Felicia was waiting there, still in her maid's outfit, since she had only brought a nightdress and an evening dress with her. A disguise was "more exciting by half anyway." Of course, Lyndell couldn't help remarking to herself, the girl naturally found a disguise exciting; Felicia looked adorable in hers! To Miss Fullerton's regret, Lyndell plunked herself down to read aloud from Miss Austen's latest novel, which she'd brought from London. The younger lady found Miss Austen prosy, much preferring Mrs. Radcliffe, or Maria Edgeworth's Gothic Tales . . .

"You know, where the beautiful heroine is always being kidnapped or ravished or thrown off a cliff. In Miss Austen they only talk. In Miss Edgeworth's books, something is always bound to happen!"

When she heard the carriage drive up, Lyndell's first thought was, Oh no, Ajax isn't even barking anymore. Her second was to remedy her disguise by snatching the spectacles out of her pocket and pulling the mob-cap down farther on her forehead. She had no time for a third as a tall, dark-haired gentleman in a stylish many-caped greatcoat filled the doorway, shouting orders: best rooms, private parlours, his cattle bedded down.

In two minutes it was as though he owned the inn. Bennett was running this way and that, yes, my lord this and right away, my lord that. Sarah was up and down the stairs, opening up doors, turning down covers, starting hot broth and warming bricks. Sam'l was put to work fetching water for the horses and even Felicia—Felicia of all people!— was told by his high and mighty lordship to run up and light the fires in the rooms. Lyndell, it appeared, was beneath the gentleman's notice; he assigned her no tasks, at any rate. Just as she was gathering her dazed thoughts for a majestic set-down, another gentleman, slighter and younger

66

than the first one's thirty years or so from what she could blurrily see, entered the doorway, supported by a servant.

"This way, Farrow," the first interloper commanded the servant, and led the way up the stairs. Before the younger man, his cheeks flushed, turned to follow, he caught a glimpse of the maid in the hall. "Fel . . ."

"Fell down, did you? Poor sir. Let me help you up the stairs." And Felicia rushed to his side, leaving Lyndell even more dumbfounded. She trailed after the cavalcade to the upper bedrooms in high dudgeon, stumbling over the bottom step.

Upstairs, the man Farrow was helping the younger gentleman out of his coat, a difficult enough task without Felicia still clutching one of his hands. Lyndell said, "The fire, Felicity" and the girl immediately ran over to the fireplace where she stood looking perplexedly at the logs, the kindling sheaf and the tinder box, without having the faintest notion of how to go on. Obviously the ninnyhammer had never started her own fire! Lyndell went to assist, just as she heard his lordship send Bennett for the doctor.

"Oh no!" Dr. Kane was sure to recognise her; he'd brought her into this world! Unfortunately, there was no hope for it, Dr. Kane being the only physician around. Even more unfortunately, she'd uttered her dismay out loud. Bennett's look was a warning, but the large gentleman's glance was only mildly curious.

"Nothing serious, ma'am, I assure you. My . . . ah . . . friend caught a chill."

"I thought he fell?"

"Well, yes, in the snow. That's how he became feverish. Damp clothes . . . Miss . . . Miss . . . ?"

"Riddley, Miss Lynn Riddley. I am in charge of this inn."

"Ah, I see. Here, Miss Riddley, perhaps we might return to the parlour so Farrow can make poor Willy more comfortable till the doctor comes. And Farrow, there seems to be some difficulty with the fire. See to it please."

Lyndell held firmly to the railing on the way down—dratted spectacles! She couldn't even get a good look at him! But his darkly handsome appearance, that aura of fearless command and the condescending politeness all convinced her that here was the villain at last! His jacket bespoke Weston, or she hadn't been on the Town for six years; the necktie tied in a Mathematical, the black curls just brushing his high collar labelled him a man of fashion; the diamond stickpin meant wealth, ill-gotten or otherwise. He'd made no demurral when Bennett addressed him as my lord, so here he was, Jasper's fine London gentleman! With an ill companion he couldn't be here for an *affaire*. Why else, then, besides evil designs?

Once in the parlour, she couldn't resist testing her supposition. "I'm surprised you didn't put up at the Golden Bell in Ipswich, sir. They would have better facilities for your horses and sick friend."

Cheyne finally took a hard look at his hostess. Gad, what a quiz! The little abigail must be as inefficient a dresser as she was a maid. Miss Riddley was totally colourless, with a slouch and an awful squint despite the spectacles. She looked like the founder of some religious order, and acted like the village busybody. He'd put an end to that presumption, at least. "Because I didn't want to answer a lot of foolish questions about Willy's injury," he told her dampeningly.

68

Aha! So he had something to hide, did he? Falling in the snow indeed! When Sarah had brought brandy and the gentleman thankfully sipped it, Lyndell took the opportunity to study him in detail, over her rims. Yes, he was the perfect scoundrel, one to make Maria Edgeworth proud: dark curls, thick unruly brows and long, nearly black lashes for a brooding look; a full mouth, firm chin, and sculpted bones for a sensual, rakish quality. Too bad his eyes were such a warm, friendly brown; they quite ruined the overall effect. Oh well, Lyndell charitably allowed, not even traitors could be totally bad. Traitor he was, though, not even commenting on the fine French brandy, after years of the blockade. Of course he wasn't surprised; he'd helped get it here.

Lyndell had to warn Captain Jamison—and get away from the inn before Bennett returned with Dr. Kane! She excused herself, made a gracious speech about hoping for his comfort at King's Pass, and made her escape, only stumbling slightly over Miss Austen's *Emma*, left lying on the floor. That was not a muffled laugh she heard; it was an evil snigger.

Chapter Eleven

"Jump, you blasted bonerattler, jump!" Kind words were not going to make the recalcitrant beast take the gate, so with an unladylike oath Lyndell got down and opened it, and it was not the first gate, either. For that matter, there was nothing ladylike at all about Miss Markham, from the buckskin breeches to the Belcher-style scarf at her neck to the beaver hat pulled low over her short fiery curls.

With Bennett gone to fetch the doctor, and Felicia encamped in the sickroom, there was no one to lend propriety to her afternoon's call on Jamison. Besides, Bennett had taken the carriage and team, leaving only a sway-backed mule and Jasper's broken down hunter, with no side-saddle at hand. Lyndell didn't hesitate for a moment, just proceeded to rummage through Jasper's clothespress. With the breeches tucked into old boots and pulled up with a belt, a fustian coat to cover her ill-fitting jacket, and the casual neckpiece, she thought she made a passable boy. Her hair was short enough, and, with the hat at a cocky angle, gave her a ragtag look she found a lot more appealing than her guise as the dreadful Miss Riddley. After the humbling experience of being an antidote, she was cheered by this jaunty lad. For a finishing touch, she used a pencil to add freckles, before creeping down the stairs and out when Mrs. Bennett's back was turned. She'd managed to saddle Riddles—the only riddle being why Jasper had bought such an iron-jawed hayburner and why he had given it a family-related name—with Sam'l's wide-eyed help, swearing him, unnecessarily perhaps, to silence. After a regretful sigh for the spy's fine cattle in their stalls, she was off. She should have taken the mule.

At first, the ride was exhilarating. Riding astride, the cold wind in her face, *ventre à terre* to report a criminal . . . this was what she'd come to Suffolk for! It didn't take long for her hardheaded realism to recover from this latest burst of fancy. Riding astride when one hadn't done it since the age of twelve was agony; the cold wind was actually a bitter dampness, chilling already protesting muscles; and riding across farming country on a steed that insisted on keeping all four feet on the ground was downright impossible. She had almost gone right over the gelding's neck at the first fence, and was forced to seek out breaks in hedgerows and crumbling sections of stone walls. What kind of hunter are you? she'd asked the dumb brute, opening yet another gate. Riddles couldn't have chased down a hedgehog, nor be it one curled in a ball! But the final, most devastating prick of her bubble of glory was at the realisation, not twenty minutes out, that she didn't know her villain's name! She could describe his broad shoulders and well-muscled thighs, the straight nose and the scar on his temple, and most of all the feeling of power about him, but could not give him a name.

Captain Jamison had been less than impressed. At first he had refused to see any Master Dell Riddley, then he was incredulous that the lad Dell should be the same person as the righteous Miss Riddley. Next he made her remove the coat and turn in front of him, to see for himself. He saw enough of rounded breast and backside to make him lick his thin, greasy lips. All of this before he'd even hear Lyndell's "evidence." While she was blushing furiously and longing to slap that leer down his hairy throat, he finally offered her a seat. She still couldn't look down her arrogant nose and turn her back on him as Miss Markham would have done; she needed this worm.

"Now Miss, or is it Master? Shall I offer Madeira or brandy?"

"Neither, thank you, and Miss will do. The disguise was necessary to deflect any suspicion a single female riding abroad would have roused."

"That's this disguise. What about the cap and glasses? Why hide your light under a bushel, hm?"

"For personal reasons that have nothing to do with this investigation which, if you could just listen, would be over shortly."

He stopped fondling his moustache. "I told you I didn't need your interference. This has nothing to do with you!"

"But it has to do with my brother Jasper."

"Ah, your . . . brother."

"Yes, my brother, who is under a great deal of suspicion while the real culprit is at the inn right now!" Noting that she finally had his attention,

Lyndell hurried on, telling all about the formidable stranger. Jamison laughed.

"You say he's strong. Was he carrying a smuggler's keg under each arm? He gives orders, so maybe he has a lot of servants. His friend's mysterious injuries? Maybe he got caught in milady's chambers, you understand?, and doesn't want it known. And as for not answering questions, let me tell you, miss, no man likes airing his linen, especially to a meddling, pushy female. You have no proof, dammit, not even a name, and you take my time with these vapourish imaginings! Leave be, ma'am."

"Then you intend doing nothing?" She jumped up, scrambling into the coat, cramming the hat on any which way.

He stayed seated, again stroking the stained bristle above his wet lips. "Now, I didn't say that, did I? I'll take a ride out tomorrow to look over this spy of yours . . . and maybe you and I can have a little, you know, private conversation too."

She knew. She turned on her heel and stomped out of the office in Jasper's too-big boots.

So there she was, cold, aching and indignant, trying to keep Riddles to a pace that would see them home before spring, if not nightfall. Shadows were bunching up around trees, and every once in a while she thought she heard another horse. Vapourish imaginings, indeed! Bushes don't form conspiracies and rabbits don't wear iron shoes and the sooner she was soaking in a hot tub, the happier she'd be.

"Come, Riddles, you can almost step over this one. Up, you—"

She would have been gratified at how easily Riddles cleared the wall if she wasn't too busy hanging on for dear life, and she would have been surprised at the frantic speed the beserking horse could maintain, if she wasn't already in a state of shock. She wasn't imagining it, they'd been shot at! That was a bullet that had whisked by her ear. If Riddles hadn't been so reluctant a jumper, she might be dead! She crouched low in the saddle, making a small target, or was that for duels! Don't panic, she told herself, the horse is doing that for you. Just hang on, even if your fingers get numb on the mane and your thighs are chafed bloody, just hang on. If you don't break your neck falling off, someone'll come along and shoot you, so just hang on!

Chapter Twelve

*H*ome! Never had a dark foul-smelling stable looked so much like heaven. Lyndell skidded off Riddles's back but kept her fingers twined in the mane. Her knuckles didn't want to unclench and her legs didn't want to hold her up. Muscles unfamiliar with riding astride be damned, it was muscles unfamiliar with being shot at. She cushioned her head on Riddles's warm sweaty neck and just stood there, trembling.

The gentleman stood by the one window in his tiny room, frowning out at the muddy rear courtyard and stable. His mind was on the next room, where Willy lay in a laudanum-induced haze. Gads, what a cock-brained thing to do, dragging him out in the cold! That Dr. Kane had clucked his disapproval, but thought a week's bed rest should see Willy fully recovered, thank goodness. At least now there was an excuse for staying on at this bedevilled hostelry, and no awkward questions from Willy, who seemed content with grinning idiotically at that little maid . . . Felicity, was it? And that was just one more small detail about this havey-cavey place he'd store away for future reflection: the stable boy who wouldn't say where his master Jasper Riddley was; that Bennett fellow scooping the doctor away nearly before he'd rolled up his bandages, and before Cheyne could ask him anything; that little chit who had a strange idea of a lady's maid's job; and that Friday-faced landlady! Most likely she'd been reading a book of sermons when he came, the exact type of self-righteous priggery he abhorred most in English womanhood. But what was she doing in this place then, at best a secluded hideaway for wayward lovers, at worst a way station for smuggled goods and stolen information, if the War Office was correct. Well, that was his job, collecting all the niggling inconsistencies and using his trained observer's instincts. He had best start soon, with that fellow riding hell-for-leather through the back woods and directly into the stable.

Lyndell's heart was beating so hard she could hear it. Oh God, it wasn't her heart, it was footsteps! It was him—the man who stole government documents . . . who may have killed a soldier . . . and whom she had just reported to the authorities! Whatever she did, she mustn't reveal her suspicions, lest he run off before Jamison get there. As matter-of-factly as possible, she tied Riddles to the crossbars, took the saddle off, and began rubbing him down. She wished she hadn't lost Jasper's hat on the mad ride home, but her hair was short enough, with luck. She wished she knew how to whistle, just a lad hard at his work, but she could not. While she was wishing, she decided, she may as well wish his lordship would check his own horses and go away. He didn't.

While Cheyne walked down the central aisle of the stable toward the horse and rider, his eyes were adjusting to the dim light from the widely spaced lanterns. Closer, he could see that the horse was dark with sweat, as if it had been running hard for some time. The rider was no more than a gangly youth, awkward in his movements, about sixteen. His face was narrow, almost delicate, saved from being effeminate only by the ridged nose and the smudges on his cheeks. In the shadowy light, the boy's hair looked carroty, and the curls were a trifle too long for fashion, most likely his proud mama's doing. When he filled out some and stopped listening to his mother, he'd be a handsome enough young man, if he lost that trapped-rabbit expression. Shy youth . . . or something to hide? To try to reassure him, and gain his confidence, Cheyne picked up a handful of straw and began rubbing the horse too.

Lyndell immediately walked behind Riddles to the other side, trying to keep the horse between her and this man whose very presence shouted *Danger*. At least, if she kept to the dark side, away from the lights, her expression mightn't tell him how horrified she was at being near a traitor. Somehow, in all her plans to save Jasper, she'd never considered holding conversation with a real criminal, even one as devastatingly handsome as this! She thought she'd take a lesson from Sam'l, too, and say nothing lest her voice give her away. So she touched her forehead in deferential acknowledgement of his presence and assistance, then lowered her head, working on Riddles's legs.

"Nice horse."

What a clanker that was, Lyndell thought. One look at his lordship's team would tell what a fine judge of horseflesh he was. One look at Riddles, the mean little eyes, the ears laid back, that flat head and short neck, would tell the merest whipster that this was not a "nice" horse. Nevertheless, she bobbed her head and said "Yessir."

"Been riding far?"

Far, as in Southwold Barracks? A simple no wasn't enough; the horse was still blowing. "Nosir, I've been teaching him to jump." A pistol shot was a novel teaching method, but it *had* worked.

Lyndell was running out of horse to rub. When the gentleman asked if she was from around the area, she could finally answer truthfully "Yessir," then she added, "I have to walk the horse, sir, he's hot," which was also true. And, she felt, a brilliant excuse to be gone from this villain's disturbing presence. Riddles, however, didn't agree. He saw his stall, he knew it was dinnertime, and he was not budging. Lyndell tugged on the lead line, pulled on it, jerked on it, while the nag glued his feet to the floor and the large gentleman looked on.

Yes, there was something decidely girlish about the lad, in spite of the nose, the marquis noted. The hands were white and slim, and there was certainly no strength in the wrists. His heavy brows lowered in thought, which Lyndell happily couldn't see, busy as she was whispering promises in Riddles's ear, if he'd only move. Then his lordship brought his hand down, hard, on Riddles's rump, and move he did, almost trampling Lyndell. She barely got the gelding out the stable door, but once out she vowed to keep walking the blasted horse till the gentleman returned to the inn, no matter how her aching legs protested.

After watching for a bit, though, Cheyne decided to stay. The gait was off—the boy's, not the horse's—and there was an ill fit to the clothes, on closer inspection, that didn't complement the cultured accents. Cheyne inspected his own horses, all bedded down nicely, and spent a few minutes stroking his own mount, Alcibiades. He considered the boy's lack of openness all of a piece, and realised he'd have a long wait, if left up to the young man. Instead he met boy and horse on a turn and walked along, one hand on Riddles's back, and continued his questions. Amazing how quickly the horse was cooled down enough! All he found out was that yes, the boy was staying at the inn, and his name was Dell—Dell something or something Dell?—before the lad had his horse back inside and in its stall, this time with Riddles's cooperation.

Lyndell thought about bolting for the inn's back door, but there was no saying this infuriating man wouldn't follow her, or hear Sarah's screams when she saw her Miss Lyndy. No, she was safer in the stable. He couldn't stay here all night, could he? And Bennett was bound to return soon, to extricate her. With Bennett gone, too, she could fill more minutes with chores, bringing hay, grain and water to Riddles, while keeping away from her nemesis, she thought.

He was there, however, taking the heavy bucket from her, asking about Jasper. She was becoming rattled, but honestly didn't know Jasper's whereabouts, so she could answer that one decisively. He was there, even closer, almost brushing against her when she filled a pail with oats, asking about the inn's clientele. And he was there, when she reached up to get a load of hay and her coat opened.

"Ah, that answers a lot of questions," he said.

Not understanding, Lyndell looked at him, then followed the direction of his eyes till she could see her own thoroughly unmannish chest straining against the white shirt. Blushing as only a redhead could, she dropped the hay and made to button Jasper's coat. A large, firm hand on her wrist stopped her. The other hand tilted her chin up. His indrawn breath gave her the only satisfaction of the whole afternoon, though why that should be, she wasn't sure. Here she was, found out by an archfiend, alone and at his mercy, and she was pleased at the obvious admiration she read in his soft brown eyes, the twitch of his lips to a smile.

Still holding her wrist with one hand as if he'd forgotten he had it, he followed the arc of her cheek, ever so gently, with his fingertips, smudging her "freckles" even worse, then traced the line of her nose. And his smile broadened, not wickedly to frighten her, but warmly, and she smiled back, staring into his eyes.

"Ah my sweet . . . Dell. Della? No, it must be Delilah, for surely you are an enchantress with those green, green eyes. But why the masquerade, love?" His smile faded, and the tiny yellow flickers stopped dancing in his eyes. "Of course, the King's Pass Inn. You're meeting your lover here!"

"Don't be foolish," was Lyndell's answer. Somehow what he thought of her was important, even if he was to be hanged shortly. Her sudden look of dismay didn't help alter his conclusion.

"Don't worry, I won't tell. No, don't bother denying it." His fingertips brushed her lips, then continued to her chin, her throat. "You're no country wench, no more than you're a schoolboy, and ladies don't frequent low taverns dressed in breeches without good reason. Unless . . ." His lopsided smile returned as Lyndell watched, nearly mesmerised by his deep voice, his steady gaze, his ever-so-whispery stroking on her neck. "Unless you're no lady."

And he drew her close with subtle pressure on her back, and tilted her head to touch her lips with his, softly at first, then with more urgency, more warmth, until Lyndell's very soul melted. Her legs, complaining for hours, finally quit completely, and she would have been a puddle at his feet if his arms hadn't held her. And still the kiss went on, teeth meeting, tongues caressing, his hands starting tremours down her back.

And yet . . . and yet she *was* a lady. She wasn't any lightskirt to be tumbled in the hay, nor an unfaithful wife taking hey-go-mad chances to meet her paramour. She wasn't any mousy old spinster either. She was, for the first time in days, Miss Lyndell Markham, a lady.

She took one step away, drew back her arm, and smashed him across the cheek with every ounce of strength her outrage lent her.

"Just who in blazes do you think you are?" she spit out.

"Cheyne," he answered, just as angrily.

"Chain, as in necklace?" she asked hopefully, but already knowing, fearing, dreading, the horrid truth:

"C-h-e-y-n-e, as in marquis."

"Good Lord!"

"I try, sweetheart, I try."

Chapter Thirteen

*H*er palm burned, her cheeks burned, and if her lips burned, well, she'd think about that later. "Don't say it," she told Mrs. Bennett, who stood letting a spoon drip on the floor, her mouth open in amazement at Lyndell's appearance. "I need a bath." She could hear her old nursemaid's jaw snap shut, before she heard a very dignified, "Yes, my lady."

Before her bath, though, Lyndell had to warn Felicia that the . . . the ogre she was running away from was here. Cheyne, the famous soldier, the profligate, the proposed bridegroom—Why, he ate children like Miss Fullerton up for breakfast.

Miss Felicia giggled. She'd known since that morning, in fact, as soon as she'd had a moment with Willy, whom she'd known forever, of course, their fathers being such good friends. Willy turned out to be Lord William Richardson, a cheerful young fribble with whom Lyndell was vaguely acquainted and whom she would now have to avoid. Another complication! At least he had sworn not to give Felicia away. He thought it a great joke to pull on his cousin who, he assured the girl, would rather marry the devil's daughter than a little peagoose like her. As for his landlady's not being all she was supposed to be, Willy knew naught of it, Felicia vowed; she'd never give her dear Miss Markham away, after all she'd done for her, and Willy was too ill to look through her disguise. Lyndell swore he'd not have the chance. She'd simply stay out of his room, which brought another matter to hand: it wasn't at all proper for Miss Fullerton to be in his lordship's bedchamber, especially if he knew she was no maidservant.

With another giggle and a quick look at Lyndell's breeches, Felicia reminded Miss Markham that propriety wasn't exactly her own long suit these days either! On her way out, she did reassure her friend that Willy was too ill to lift his head, much less threaten her virtue. Oh, and yes, she'd certainly steer clear of Cheyne, without any urging. The man was dangerous.

How dangerous, Felicia would never know, Lyndell hoped. She didn't have a chance to pursue that thought, either, as Bennett came in just then, toting two cans of hot water and wanting to know what she'd done to put his Sarah in such a swivet. One look at the breeches made him smile, but when Lyndell told him how she'd ridden to warn Captain Jamison of the traitor, his craggy face seamed up in a grin and he slapped his knee. Tears were streaming from his eyes, it was such a good joke. His Miss Lyndy riding cross-country on a plug to turn in one of the most heroic veterans of the Peninsular campaign. Aside from Cheyne's being one of Wellington's hand-picked aides, entrusted with carrying the most secret orders of the whole war, he'd been out of the country till two months ago, as any lobcock who read the papers knew. All she'd had to do was check the ledger, the very same one she'd told Bennett to fetch out, and she would have saved herself a peck of trouble. As for the gunshot, Bennett pooh-poohed it. Just poachers undoubtedly, and nowhere near her. Shots just sounded close in the dark. Bennett couldn't wait to go tell Sarah how Miss Lyndy'd left her wits in London.

At least she'd given her friends something to laugh about, Lyndell thought ruefully as she lowered her poor sore body into the tub. Her legs were still like porridge, and the top layer of skin gone, stuck to Jasper's breeches. And her lips . . .

She sank down lower, shut her eyes, and, her fingers to her lips, recalled that kiss. It wasn't her first kiss by any means, not at twenty-four, but the others had been flirtatious, suggestive, quick and, well, cool. None had left her with more than a mild curiosity, or a pleasant tingle; none had left this heat, minutes later. And the warmth wasn't just in her lips, she recalled, and remembering, felt it again. At last, after reading all those books where the heroine felt a fire in her loins, Lyndell knew where her loins were! What a world of difference there was between pleasant and passionate, for though she'd never known passion before, she recognised it instantly.

Too bad its instigator was such a rogue, she thought dreamily, even if he wasn't a spy. If he wasn't a spy, how far could coincidence stretch to bring him to the inn? There was Felicia, but she'd been blown off course; what would Cheyne's excuse be for leaving the main roads, the major posting inns, unless Willy had urged him here? Unless William Richardson, the carefree young Corinthian, was the traitor. . . .

She'd made enough wretched errors for one day. Right now she wanted to think of the marquis. He was an unprincipled rake who took advantage of young girls, but he'd let her go the moment she protested. He was a practised seducer, but she'd let herself be entranced by his voice, his touch, his eyes. He was dangerous. Persistent in pursuit, wickedly observant, and he could ruin her if he knew her name. Dell Riddley had to disappear for good, and Miss Lynn Riddley had to avoid the gentleman like the plague, much to Miss Markham's regret. There it was, as plain as the raw places on her legs: for all his knavery, the indignity and outrage of his behaviour, Lyndell's major emotion, besides the one felt in her new-found loins, was one of relief that the Marquis of Cheyne wasn't her villain after all. And if he wasn't the villain . . .

On her way to dinner, scurrying past the closed front parlour door, Miss Riddley paused, however belatedly, to inspect the ledger, open on the hall table in the innkeeper's niche under the stair. There it was, by the oil lamp's light, in sure, firm letters, *Cheyne, et al.* She touched the signature briefly in what, for a middle-aged spinster, was a remarkably romantic gesture, before hurrying on to the kitchen.

Sarah was still disgruntled, more so when Felicia begged to be allowed to bring the younger lord his supper. Lyndell sided with the girl, especially since that would free the man Farrow to wait on his own master, getting the manservant out of the kitchen too. Lyndell had to talk to Bennett. It was imperative he go up to King's Mark that very night and search out Jasper. She urged him to try the unused grooms' quarters over the stables, or the gatekeeper's cottage, for Jasper had used to be a favourite of old Diccon.

With Bennett gone, though, Lyndell couldn't just flee to her own sitting room where she and her thoughts would be safe. She had to bide downstairs, in case any travellers came. Molly could handle the tap room customers, and Sam'l could take care of the horses, but if someone wanted a room, which they might, the weather not worsening any, Lyndell had to be at hand.

That's why she was still in the kitchen when Dr. Kane returned to check on his patient and see if perhaps Mrs. Bennett had any of those Bath buns left over. Sarah introduced Miss Riddley, of course, but the old doctor just said "Hmm," giving her a good look.

"There's those that can be fooled, and then again, there's those that can't." He held up his hand to stop any disclaimers. "Take me for instance. Now I know better'n any that Elvira Riddley had no daughter; I birthed Jasper myself, and another stillborn babe that she died bearing. Then again, I'd never heard of the Earl of Markham leaving his butter stamp about the countryside." At Mrs. Bennett's reproachful tsks, he cleared his throat. "Now I'm not putting my nose"—he chuckled at his own wit—"in anyone else's business, but I'd suggest, miss, that I'm not the only one with eyes in my head."

There was only one set of travellers that evening before Bennett returned: *Mr. and Mrs. Blackburn*, the man wrote in the hall ledger, requesting adjoining bedrooms. No maid, no valet, no baggage. They were so busy staring into each other's eyes they gave the dreary landlady no second glance. Lyndell, however, even in the light of the single lamp she'd let burn in the hall, recognised them instantly: Lord Naybors, he of the wife and sickly children, and Sophie Davenant, whose husband was in Vienna with the diplomatic corps.

Naybors she put in Room Ten, across from Cheyne. Sophie Davenant she put in Room One, across from Molly. And let that be an object lesson, my fine lady.

Chapter Fourteen

Cheyne saw the Blackburns come in. If those two were married he was the King of Persia, but he went back to his dinner of good English country fare. A short while later he heard Mr. Blackburn expostulating over the room arrangements with Miss Riddley, and he grinned. Just like an old prune, if she wasn't going to enjoy herself, no one else was going to enjoy himself. And anything less likely than Miss Riddley enjoying herself—much less in a bedroom with a man—was hard to imagine. Quite unlike his little temptress of the afternoon, he thought, rubbing his slightly swollen cheek. She actually was not so little for a woman, and not quite in the first blush of youth, but she was certainly no milk-and-water miss. He couldn't help smiling in remembrance of her spirit, no more than he could forget the sweetness of her kiss. But who in hell was she? The one-page-old ledger had yielded no information, he and Willy being the only recorded guests, and a quick look showed the rooms near theirs untenanted. He knew she was still in the inn, since her gelding was still in the stable; he'd checked. But he couldn't very well go opening every door down the corridor. Well, he would, if he was sure Miss Riddley wouldn't catch him at it. Cheyne didn't think the girl could be a servant, not when she stood right up to him that way, but that only left a connexion with Riddley or his sister. Miss Riddley was out. What could she have to do with a hoydenish, glorious, green-eyed witch? On the other hand, the idea of his Delilah with that loose screw Riddley soured his wine. He'd just have to wait to puzzle out his mystery woman, along with the rest of this mess.

Damn the War Department anyway. Just go look around, they'd said. The usual thing, there's a good fellow. Well, this wasn't the usual thing, not by a sow's tail. He'd expected to deal firmly with Riddley, talk sociably to the locals, find what he needed, and straighten it out. Instead, he was enmeshed in some deuced petticoat intrigue! Women! And the list of the creatures was growing; even the doctor grumbling about misplaced chits. But which? There was the prudish Miss Riddley who turned down corners when she saw him coming. Her skitterwitted little maid, who had taken to blushing and squeaking in his presence, though she seemed rational enough with Willy, for which Cheyne would have to berate his cousin. The chit was a regular pocket Venus, but gads, a lady's maid! If Willy was too ill to take what she was offering, why was he making sheep-eyes at her in his every waking moment? The boy definitely needed a nice, respectable wife to take him in hand. Then there was the mysterious visitor in the stable, his Delilah. The possessive seemed to come as natural as breathing. Lastly there was Molly, the barmaid, who was the only one of the bunch to show him any friendliness. Right then a little friendliness seemed not such a bad thing. It had been a long day, starting way before the nightmare of Willy's accident in the snow. Besides, Molly was the likeliest source of information he was going to find this long, cold night. Sitting alone in the private parlour with his port— damn fine port too—thinking about Willy lying there in the snow bleeding, or a pair of green eyes sparkling with passion's fire, wasn't going to solve anything. He carried his bottle, now three-quarters empty, and the glass into the common room.

The man Bennett was back from wherever he'd ridden off to earlier. That was one of the most closed-mouthed chaps the marquis had come up against, off on an errand instead of giving an answer every time. The stableboy was worse. Who ever heard of a barn brat not taking a bribe for some information? If Cheyne hadn't heard Bennett call the lad, he'd not even know his name. But there was Molly, with her voluptuous bosom and yellow hair, winking at him as she brought tankards over to a pair of workingmen, swinging her hips in exaggerated motion on her way back to the bar.

Cheyne set his bottle down on a table near the men, in case their talk should yield any clues. All he heard though was, "What's old Molly after now, awaggin' her tail like a bitch in heat?"

"Not for you, you old gaffer. Finer feathers nor yours, she has in mind, I figure." And the speaker nudged his companion in Cheyne's direction. The marquis raised his glass in acknowledgement, hoping to encourage the men's familiarity, but they just turned back to their ale and their talk of fixing the roads, come spring.

Cheyne's bottle finished, he signalled for the barkeep who came over, wiping his hands on his apron. Before the marquis could even hint at a question, however, Bennett informed him that Molly would be taking over now, as Bennett had to be up with the horses in the morning. Anything his Lordship wanted, just ask Molly, he said, leaving. Aye, a knowing one was that Bennett, with the look of a horse trader in his eye.

Molly brought him another bottle. Fine French Burgundy this time. She managed to rub against his shoulder putting the bottle down, and gave him a generous view of her admirable cleavage leaning over to wipe at the table.

"Excellent wine you serve here," he mentioned casually. "I wonder if there'd be any way I could purchase a case or so to take home with me."

"Well, I don't know, love. Jasper usually handles that 'n there's no telling when he'll be back."

"Surely you could procure me a few bottles at least, couldn't you?"

"Mayhap I could, if it was, you know, worth my while."

"And what would it take"—laughing brown eyes looked at her over the rim of his glass—"to make it worth your while?"

"I'll have to think on it," she said, going over to settle the farmers' accounts. "Maybe we could talk about it later."

Cheyne had another glass. Then another, while the workers put on their heavy overcoats, their mufflers, their mittens. Finally Molly came back to him, and he merely had to hold an arm out to have her in his lap. Like the gentleman he was, he offered her some of his wine. "Don't mind if I do; not many of the customers offer the good stuff. You're a real fine gent, you are."

With a little snuggling and some friendly fondling and as much wine as it took, he hoped to find out just where this Jasper was, where the wine came from and who her other gentlemen friends were. When she started nibbling on his ear and shivering, saying what a cold night it was, with the downstairs fire put out and all, he knew the lady wasn't giving anything away free. When her hands started roving lower, and she mentioned that maybe, just maybe, she could find the name of Jasper's wine dealer, upstairs, Cheyne decided to make the supreme sacrifice. For God and country.

"I have to lock up down here, love. Go left at the top of the stairs; it's the last door on the left."

Willy was sleeping peacefully when Cheyne looked in on him, Farrow dozing in a chair next to the bed. He'd have to make it up to poor Farrow, but at least the goosish maid wasn't spending the night! He went back to his own room and undressed, putting on only a paisley silk dressing gown and a lopsided smile . . . all in the line of duty, sir. He took a candle with him as he padded to the door in his bare feet, then came back and stuffed a few pound notes in his pocket.

At this moment, the marquis's thinking wasn't quite at par with the battle-heightened acumen for which he was famous. He'd been without sleep for well over two days, and had been living at a fast pace for months before. He'd had too much to drink tonight, and every night this week. He'd had the shock of Willy's accident, his own remorse, and the affecting incident in the stable. In other words, his wits were gone begging. What he was using for brains at this moment was located entirely elsewhere.

Therefore, when he reached the top of the stairs, he went left, and continued on to the last door on the left, just like Molly had said. Of course Molly's directions were from the bottom of the stairs, looking up, not from his room near the central hall.

There was no answer when he scratched softly on the door. Maybe Molly was still closing up, in which case he could do a little snooping, though he didn't really expect to find contraband goods hidden beneath her bed. The door he opened showed a room in darkness, except for snow-reflected moonlight through the rear window. It appeared to be a small sitting room with two equally dark bedchambers to either side. The nearest bedchamber, he could see by his candle's light, was obviously a man's, with jackets, boots, harness pieces, and neckcloths strewn about. It didn't take much to deduce that the missing tenant was also the disappeared innkeeper, Riddley. The room was too cluttered for any transient guest, and its corner location gave the best vantage of both the roadway and the stableyard. If this was Jasper's chamber, the other must be Molly's. It followed, to Cheyne's reasoning, that Molly was therefore Riddley's mistress, and his estimation of that gentleman, not high to start, dropped another notch. Not because Riddley had a mistress, not even because she was a rustic like Molly, but that he'd share her with anyone with the price. Unless, of course, Riddley didn't know. It didn't matter a ha'penny. What did was that if

Molly shared Riddley's suite, and his bed, Delilah didn't!

With that tortuous reasoning concluded, Cheyne realised his candle was burning low and his bare feet were getting chilled and he could barely keep his eyes open. He could light the fire in the sitting room, offering Molly a chance to sit and chat, when she came up, or he could wait for her under the covers. Major Richardson of the Fourth Cavalry would have braved the elements and put aside personal considerations, for the cause. Wesley Richardson, Fifth Marquis of Cheyne, after his second bottle and after bruising his toes on a pile of books, chose the bed.

Molly's bedroom was smaller than Riddley's, very austere by comparison. Surprisingly, there was nothing lying about except there on the bed. "Molly?" he whispered. He got no answer, but obviously she was there before him, playing coy. It seemed there'd be no genial conversation first, after all. Trying to feel regretful that it was to be pleasure before business, and failing, the marquis placed his candle on the dressing table. Then as noisily as he could, he uncrinkled the pound notes from his pocket and placed them under the candleholder, to show he understood the game. He dropped his dressing gown on the side of the bed and got in. The light was even poorer—the moon must be cloud-covered—and his candle was on the other side of the room, so he could barely make out the light curls on the pillow, and he only vaguely noted that the figure under the blankets didn't seem quite what the satin bodice had promised.

Moving closer, he called "Molly" again, and chuckled at her silence. He gently kissed one eyelid and then the other, and placed one of his hands on her breast. The eyelids snapped open.

Cheyne was just considering how this wondrously soft, warm, rounded breast had appeared so . . . so flabby earlier, when a voice hissed in his ear: "It's you!"

"Of course it is, sweetings, you invited me," he answered and covered her mouth with his. This was no tentative kiss, nor sweetly intense. It was hard and demanding, with a fiery tongue. It vibrated with the intent to arouse her to passion. And it succeeded. With one arm she gave him a shove and with the other arm Lyndell gave him another clout on the side of his head.

"I never did, you . . . you libertine!"

The marquis sat up in horror. My God, he thought. It's the landlady! But no . . . he couldn't see the red-gold of her hair, or the green eyes he was sure were smouldering, but there in the unreliable light of the moon was that same profile, that same nose, and yes, it had been that same roundhouse right. Thank heavens!

"Get out, you reprobate, you ravisher, you—"

He got out of her bed before she had the whole house out of theirs, and stood there, trying to apologise. "I . . . I thought you were Molly, you see . . ."

What she saw, in that same moonlight haze, was *his* profile, and evidence that his interest, so to speak, was at the highest. She screeched one more "Get out, you evil man" while pulling the blankets over her head.

Not even when the enemy had charged Valdoz had the marquis moved so fast. He was out of the sitting room, stubbing his toes again, and on the other side of the door before he had his sash tied, and before Lord Naybors had closed his own door, down the hall.

By Jupiter, Naybors gasped, Cheyne and the landlady! That's bravery indeed!

Chapter Fifteen

The first thing Lyndell did the next morning, after unbarricading her door, was have it out with Molly: No flirting with the customers. No painted lips or low-cut dresses. And no men in her bedroom.

"If you're worried about your 'tips,' you will now be receiving a salary." Lyndell smacked Cheyne's five pound notes down on the dresser. "Here's your first payment."

Gads, was all Molly could think of, roused so roughly from her sleep to hear her employer's diatribe. What had Miss Prunes-and-Prisms in such a pelter now? She wiped her eyes. Then, as her mind started to wake up too, she recalled last night's ruckus, and began to laugh.

"So that's what happened to his nibs! What a shock he must have had!" She took in Lyndell's shapeless navy wool gown and the limp cap and laughed even louder. "There's not many women I know as would throw such a handsome buck out of their beds."

"I don't doubt that for a minute," was Lyndell's retort as she slammed the door behind her, leaving Molly flushed with hilarity at the ways of the gentry.

Miss Markham was furious. She was burning, and this time it wasn't with passion. It *was* physical yearning, to be sure, an intense desire to box that lecher's ears. Hang the molester up by his thumbs! Pull out every one of those shiny black curls!

It wasn't just the kiss, though that was bad enough. The kiss itself was actually one of the more stirring moments of her life. She'd never been kissed lying down, and there was a big difference, she'd found. That wasn't the point, however. The rake had come unbidden into her rooms in the middle of the night, assaulted her virtue and, the supreme insult, apologised for mistaking her for Molly! Boiling in oil was too good for the dastard.

What she needed right now was Jasper: Jasper coming forward with his evidence, even confessing his part in the smuggling if he had to. Then Lyndell could go home, taking the innocent Miss Fullerton out of the old goat's way. What she needed was Jasper to lend her countenance. Much as she deplored the fact, a woman under her brother's or father's or husband's protection was less likely to be harassed, which was why proper ladies were never unescorted. Even if she couldn't see clear to her weakling step-brother's defending her honour against such a virile man as the marquis, she needed his actual presence.

What she got, however, was Bennett's report that yes, he'd located Jasper, and yes, he was hiding out with old Diccon, in the gatehouse attics where he'd go undetected. And no, he would not return to the inn. Jasper felt he did not have enough information to go to the authorities with, Bennett gloomily reported, but he knew too much of the goings-on for the criminals' safety. If he wasn't arrested, he'd be killed, so he was not budging. Unless, of course, Lyndell was willing to lay down the blunt to see him safely out of the country. She considered it, then discarded the idea. His name—and hers—would still have the tarnish on it, even more so if the mess was never resolved. She'd see the lily-livered coward out of the country, all right, but not yet.

The first thing the marquis did when he awoke, after laying a cool cloth on his aching head, was to see how Willy was doing. His cousin seemed to be making a great recovery, grinning like a cat in the cream, while the little maid spooned porridge into him. As if his arm was hurt, and not his foot, Cheyne fumed. Still a little warm to the touch, Willy was in high fettle, but the girl, Felicity, was even more clothheaded then usual. Instead of blushing, as she had previously, now she jumped up and ran to the other side of the bed, spilling hot gruel on her poor patient.

It was Cheyne's turn to blush; obviously the chit had been warned of his own wanton lust. And here he'd been about to chide Willy for dallying with a maid! His own actions looked even worse by daylight. What was he about, making great gaffes like that, nearly ravishing innocent maids? Of course his maid wasn't quite the innocent, not if she was in Jasper Riddley's keeping. Yet there was something so pure about her kisses, and she'd seemed so sweetly willing, up to a point. If he hadn't had such a weathered tan, his cheek would be a discoloured yellow by now. That was the point. At least she wasn't a lady, thank God, with duennas and chaperones and ten male relatives clamouring for his blood. He could just see some stiff-rumped baronet demanding satisfaction unless he married the girl. But a lightskirt?

He'd apologise, possibly buy her a gift if there was a store in the village with some gewgaws, a fan or parasol perhaps, and that would be that. After all, not much had actually happened, certainly not as much as he wished! In order to apologise he had to find her, but without knocking on the door he knew would be locked to him. He didn't even know her name, really, or what she was doing here. For that matter, he didn't know what *he* was doing here!

He had to do better than this, he told himself. Where was all that vaunted intellect, the perspicacity that had kept him alive through all those years of war? If he couldn't untangle this little inn's messy web, he'd be ashamed to face the general again.

"This is the most ramshackle hostelry it has even been my misfortune to visit. Poor rooms, discourteous service, midnight carryings-on. This is the last you'll have of my custom, Miss Riddley, and I'll be certain to tell all my friends. Good day."

Good riddance to bad rubbish, Mr. Blackburn, Lyndell thought, nearly biting her tongue to keep herself from sending regards to Lady Naybors. No sense in drawing attention, nor in speaking more than she had to, lest he think her voice was familiar. Yet it was remarkable, Lyndell thought, how little people really noticed, especially the upper classes. If you weren't fashionable, or good *ton*, you barely existed. Just by wearing unfashionable gowns, a cap and spectacles, she faded right into the background. Cheyne had barely nodded to her when they met; Naybors felt he could treat her like a servant; Jamison like a half-wit. A Mrs. Cox, in ermine and emeralds, took one look at Miss Riddley, the squint, the stoop, and requested her rooms through her maid, as if she needed an interpreter. Of course, when a Mr. Bushnell arrived, in corsets and eye-threatening shirtpoints, asking for a room next to his sister, Mrs. Cox, Miss Riddley-the-nonentity took great pleasure in announcing that the inn was full.

Lyndell was wrong, at least about the marquis. At the moment he was very much interested in her. He had just finished shaving and was about to tie the neckcloth Farrow had handed him when a commotion of shouts and snarls and screams in the stable yard below drew him to the window. His first thought on seeing the crowd of people out there was that his red-haired vixen wasn't one of them. His next thought was that with the drab Miss Riddley outside, it was a good time to search the rest of the upstairs rooms. But what in the blazes were those people doing out there? Bennett was holding a pistol, in a very businesslike way. Mrs. Bennett was doing the screaming, flapping a blanket in the air. The sulky stableboy had a jar of something, and Miss Riddley, wielding a large knife, was advancing on a mangy cur that was growling and snapping. The marquis left without tieing his neckcloth.

* * *

It vaguely registered in Cheyne's mind that Miss Riddley wasn't wearing her spectacles, but his attention was focussed on the dog. Bennett explained the situation to him, in the most pessimistic of terms, and the marquis assumed charge. He took the blanket from Mrs. Bennett, admonishing her to be still, lest she upset the poor beast further.

"Bennett, do you know how to use that thing?"

"Aye, well enough."

"Let's hope so," the marquis said, advancing closer to Miss Riddley and the dog Ajax, the blanket loosely wrapped around one arm. "Miss Riddley, do stand to the side more, that's it, out of Bennett's line of fire. Right. You, sir," to Ajax, "stop that noise. Down, Ajax!"

Ajax was weak, and terrified of all the people surrounding him, but he heard that voice of authority, the same firm voice used to give orders to the greenest of raw recruits. He was not conceding to it yet, certainly not lying down to be kicked or beaten or whatever, but he did stop lurching about. The marquis approached touching distance.

"Miss Riddley, at the count of three, you will clap your hands and shout, to get his attention. One . . . two . . . three." As Ajax turned to the new threat, the marquis made his move. With one fluid motion he had an arm around the animal's neck and the other hand firmly encircling the dog's mouth, keeping those jaws tightly shut. Ajax whined and struggled to get away, but the marquis's grip was like iron. "Good fellow, steady there. Now Miss Riddley, whilst I hold the mouth, take the blanket—no, take my neckcloth. Tie it firmly about his snout."

Lyndell did as she was told, having to come closer still to remove the white linen from his neck. She was blushing furiously, but luckily Cheyne was concentrating on the dog. She had to brush his fingers with hers, wrapping the cloth. Hers trembled; his were strong, brown, unmoving. She lapped the cloth two or three times around the beast's jaws before the marquis directed her to tie a knot, tightly, behind Ajax's head, "So he can't just scratch the muzzle off."

When that was done, the marquis was able to shift his position for a better grip on the dog's body while Lyndell attempted to cut the rope on his neck. The cord was too deeply embedded, however, the raw oozing skin having swelled about it. Both Lyndell and Cheyne were kneeling in the mud of the yard, his buckskins and her navy skirt fouled now, and she felt like weeping with frustration. "I can't do it without cutting his skin! Oh Ajax, I'm so sorry." Without loosening his hold, the marquis inspected this new problem. Then he turned to Sam'l. "You, boy. Go ask my man Farrow for my shaving razor. Quick now."

Sam'l stood there, rooted in the mud, looking at Lyndell beseechingly. "Sam'l . . . he doesn't talk much, my lord," she told the marquis in a low voice. "We think he was beaten too."

"Damn," with feeling. "But I can't hold the mutt forever. Bennett, can you—" But Sam'l was gone, running into the inn.

While they waited, Lyndell tried to soothe Ajax, stroking his ears, talking softly. Her arm touched the marquis's hand and he looked up. "You're not wearing your spectacles."

"No. I don't . . . that is, sometimes . . ." Giving it up, she took them out of her pocket and put them on, but not before Cheyne had seen green eyes, as clear as sunlight on a spring leaf. With the lenses the eyes seemed blurry, cloudy. Maybe he just had emerald eyes on his mind. No, there, right where the glasses sat on the bridge of her nose, a bump, a ridge . . .

The razor was thrust at him by a grinning Sam'l. "Good lad! Now, ma'am, let's do it before my arm goes numb." If he noticed that she removed the glasses before starting, he didn't comment. "Watch, the blade is sharp. That's it."

At last the rope was off. Sam'l brought the jar of salve Bennett had found in the stable and Lyndell slathered it on Ajax. Shrugging, she wiped her hand on her skirt, already trailing in the muck. She looked up to catch a one-sided almost-smile on Cheyne's handsome face. Embarrassed, she looked down at Ajax. "Now what, my lord?"

"Now comes the tricky part. We must remove the muzzle, without getting bitten, of course, then get him to a place where he can't run away. The stable?"

"Of course. Sam'l, take a blanket and make Ajax a bed in one of the loose boxes—lots of straw so he doesn't get a chill."

"Right. Now, ma'am, undo the knot, but don't loosen the cloth until I have my hand on his jaws again . . . there. I have him. Good Ajax."

With both hands around considerable poundage of dog, the marquis was getting up slowly. Bennett started to come forward in assistance, which caused Ajax to start struggling again. Cheyne ordered Bennett to back off. With a deep breath, the marquis stood up, Ajax in his arms. When he staggered a bit, Lyndell steadied his elbow with her hand—it seemed the thing to do—and so they made their slow way into the stable.

The marquis was covered with dirt and dog hairs

and breathing heavily, but Ajax was in his stall, with Sam'l offering him a bowl of water.

"He'll do, I think," the marquis told Lyndell. He was trying to study her face, but the stable was dark, and his eyes were not adjusted from the morning's sunlight outside. Besides, she had the blasted spectacles on again, and her head down. If only she wasn't wearing that atrocious cap! There was a definite similarity. He was positive of it. It was hard to think of any relation between his vibrant Delilah and the inflexible Miss Riddley— sisters? By Jupiter, maybe his nymph was Miss Riddley's by-blow? The lady had unbent some in the stable yard, and she'd certainly shown great fortitude. What she'd been trying to do may have been foolhardy, but it had taken more courage and generosity of spirit than he'd seen in most ladies of his acquaintance.

He tried to tell her so, though the governessy Miss Riddley couldn't even take a compliment. No practise, obviously. She stiffly thanked him for his impressive actions, awkwardly twisting the neckcloth she still held in her hands, not meeting his eyes. She would give Mrs. Bennett the cloth to be laundered, and was terribly sorry for the inconvenience, sincerest appreciation—and she was gone, nearly bumping into the center beam of the barn.

The marquis stayed in the stable a long while after, thinking.

Chapter Sixteen

*W*hy did that dratted man have to be so charming? Here she thought he'd sleep until noon like all the Bond Street beaux. She knew for a fact he hadn't been to bed early. She hadn't even considered that she might encounter him, thus the missing spectacles, while he'd been up at first light, like a soldier off to battle! If his sole purpose was to torment her, he was doing a fine job! How dare he be so cool and efficient with Ajax, so kind and gentle with Sam'l, so damned polite to Miss Riddley! Somehow she couldn't regain her indignation of the morning. Of course, she told herself, that's what made a rake: a lack of scruples sugar-coated with appeal. If a rake couldn't make a girl's heart beat faster, he was no good at the job. The marquis was very good at it, lurking in the corridors, seeking her out in the kitchen, watching her with that lazy smile. The man was a positive hazard to womankind! She managed to avoid him, staying occupied with the inn's business. Saturday was market day in Entwood, so the livestock dealers, merchants and well-to-do farmers from farther away stopped in for their suppers, with some bespeaking rooms for the night. A few London visitors came through, as out of place as peacocks in the chicken coop.

"Lord Beaumont and Lady Anabelle Beaumont, a room for the night? Let me see." That was Lord Beaumont, all right, all twenty stone of him, and his companion nearly matched him in girth. Lady Ann, however, a good friend of Lyndell's Aunt Hardesty, was a tiny wraith of a woman.

"I'm afraid Number Four is the only room available. Market day, you know.

Room Number Four was a converted dressing room, equipped for a servant, valet or maid. It contained one extremely narrow bed.

The Bennetts had agreed: it was better to run an honest inn where decent people would stay than to make a profit on sordid assignations. Sarah was especially vehement: she wasn't having such goings-on under her roof! Let them sleep in the fields like animals if that was how they conducted themselves. Silk waistcoats and lace smallclothes—and no better nor rabbits. The only question was, would they also be turning away the man they were waiting for? What if he were clever enough to mask his true motives with a ladybird? Lyndell thought that if his business at the inn was important enough, he'd make certain he stayed. Bennett agreed.

"Squire Asgar and family? Welcome to King's Pass. We have a lovely suite with a sitting room, and I'm sure Mrs. Bennett has some gingerbread for the children."

"Captain Drew Jamison?" Gads, she'd forgotten all about him! Here he was, come to arrest a spy, and all she had was one silver-tongued devil with a scar on his forehead. The only traitor was the flutter in her heart.

"Captain Jamison, I meant to send a message, but we've been so busy. The thing is, the man I thought was the saboteur couldn't be him. He—"

"Come, ma'am, let's just see the blighter and be done. Then you and I can have a little *tête-a-tête*, hmm?" He winked. Lyndell excused herself, flew up the stairs and demanded Felicity's presence in the front parlour. "Do not leave me alone with that man!"

"Which man?"

"Either of them! Bring tea or something, but hurry!"

She took a deep breath before returning to lead the captain to the parlour. Before the marquis said "Come in" to her knock, she thought of developing a sudden headache, but Jamison had her elbow and was propelling her inside. The Marquis was at ease by the fire, reading a book. He'd changed his soiled buckskins for buff-coloured pantaloons, and his cravat was tied—

He caught her looking at it. "I call it the Ajax Knot," he told her, getting to his feet and smiling. Then he noticed the man behind her and the smile died. "Captain Jamison."

"Major." Jamison saluted.

Heavens, thought Lyndell, they were friends!

"Not major," Cheyne corrected, motioning them to seats. "I sold out some months ago. Time to settle down. And what of your plans, Drew, do you intend to stay on now that the war's over?"

"Aye, I'll stay. Some of us aren't so fortunate to have estates to fall back on."

"As you say. Well, what brings you here? Are you still at Southwold? Will you have some wine, Miss Riddley? Drew?"

Reminded of her presence, Jamison turned to look at Miss Riddley, who was busily wiping her spectacles. Jamison stared at her, then back at the marquis, then burst into loud snorts of laughter. Cheyne raised one dark eyebrow.

"I thought, that is, I felt—" Lyndell began, ready to confess her suspicions. The eyebrow rose higher.

"Miss Riddley thought you might wish to see an old acquaintance, Cheyne. I heard you were in the vicinity so I decided to call. By the way, we've had a bit of a problem in the neighbourhood. Don't suppose you've heard about it?"

The marquis inspected the tassle on his Hessians. "No, nothing. I have been too busy in London to take an interest." At Jamison's knowing leer, he continued, "But what's the trouble? Perhaps I can help. I did have a lot of behind-the-lines experience, you know."

"No, no, nothing to concern yourself about. Highwaymen, most likely." Jamison looked sideways at Lyndell. "You know how females are, though. They fret and fidget. Delicate nerves."

If Cheyne had his own suspicions about the scowling Miss Riddley, they did not include dieaway airs. He surprised himself by resenting Jamison's slurs. What he really resented, he realised, was the coxcomb's leering familiarity with her. With the straight-laced Miss Riddley? *No one* would flirt with Miss Riddley unless . . .

To Lyndell's relief, Felicity brought the tea tray. She bobbed a curtsey, rattling the china, before

Lyndell could take it from her. "Do not leave," Lyndell whispered. Jamison transferred his ogling to the pretty little maid—Cheyne had his suspicions about that too—while Miss Riddley fussed with asking the gentlemen's preferences. Felicity passed the muffins.

When Jamison had his cup, his moustache dripping tea down the front of his uniform, to Lyndell's disgust, he asked the marquis, "So what brings you here, hm?" His damp eyes went from Miss Riddley to her maid; his tone was one of heavy-handed insinuation. Presumptuous ass, though Cheyne, before his quirky sense of humour took over. This was as good a time as any to put one of his theories to the test. A spark of deviltry lighting his smile, he answered: "I'm going north on an errand for my uncle. Viscount Richardson, you recall. Looking over some prime breeding stock."

Lyndell gasped. Miss Fullerton, however, tossed the plate of pastries in the air and fled.

Muffins rolled under the chairs, muffins trailed crumbs over the carpets. If Lyndell had her way, his lordship would have a muffin crammed down his throat! It looked as though he was already choking, but on a smothered laugh. "Dratted girl," was all she said, staring significantly at him, so he would know who else was in her black book. Who knew what else he might say? For that matter, who knew what else he suspected? She had to keep him away from Jamison at all costs now, lest he feel inclined to explain the maid's dismay or, worse, compare notes on one Dell Riddley. "I'm sure you're anxious to return to your men, Captain. You mentioned a private matter . . . ?" Her stomach almost turned at the thought.

Instead of leading him back down the hall, or to

a corner of the nearly empty common room, she went out the front door, near where his horse was tied. Surprisingly, there were no other men waiting. Had he come to make the arrest single-handedly? Either way, this was going to be a brief conversation, if she had anything to say about it.

Jamison dropped his oily urbanity the moment they were outside. "What do you mean, dragging me out here? Master spies . . . London gentlemen? Wellington's right-hand man, more like it! I don't know what game you're playing, missy, and I won't have it! No one plays Drew Jamison for a fool."

"No, no. You don't understand. It was an error, I tried to tell you. But . . . but his cousin is here, with some odd tale of a wound. He could be the one." Lyndell didn't really believe it, though she tried to sound convincing. Willy Richardson, that devil-may-care park saunterer? Absurd.

"Proof, ma'am, I need proof!" He seized her hand. "See that you don't make any more errors, and stay out of what don't concern you. I'll return another time, when his lordship"—with a sneer—"isn't watching." He indicated the window, where Cheyne's broad shoulders were framed. Then he lifted her hand and kissed the palm of it. "For our little talk."

Cheyne saw the gesture. Miss Riddley and that cad Jamison? From what his directives mentioned, that meant she was in it up to her eyes after all. Too bad, and he'd dared to hope that his theories were correct. Foolish notion, of course. Damn. He did not see Miss Riddley furiously rubbing her hand off on her skirt. And neither one, naturally, was aware of Jamison's moustache-stroking deliberations, once back at the barracks. Crumbs fell on the page in front of him as he hastily wrote: "Cheyne here. Did the War Office send him? What now?"

"Mr. and Mrs. . . . Jones? Yes, we ought to be able to accommodate you. I'll just go see if the rat-catcher is finished. . . . You've decided to push on after all? Perhaps another time . . ."

When Cheyne asked Miss Riddley to dine with him, she could find no gracious way to refuse. He was to spend a week there, he pleaded, and his own company was already beginning to tire him. With Farrow and the maid seeing so well to Willy's comfort, there was nothing to occupy him. The parlour door would remain open, of course.

Lyndell didn't recall being so nervous since she'd curtsied to the queen, wearing those clumsy hoops and crinolines. Now she was dressed in cast-offs, but at least she didn't wear the spectacles. He'd already seen her without them, and, aside from the danger of spilling her soup, she needed all her senses about her. She could barely remember whom she had told which lies to, and he was such a . . . a knowing one, despite those friendly eyes. She squared her shoulders. Miss Markham had been giving set-downs for years, and Miss Riddley was certainly stiff-rumped enough to deflect any personal question. It was only the lad Dell Riddley she had to worry about.

To her relief, dinner was actually pleasant. Instead of the inquisition she'd expected, there was polite conversation. No mention was made of Jamison's visit, Felicity's awkwardness, the missing Jasper, or, thank goodness, Dell Riddley. Lyndell was at ease over the braised veal and the turbot in oyster sauce, enjoying the marquis's company. He'd changed for dinner into black knee pants and a perfectly fitted coat of blue superfine, and his manners were superb. Polite without being encroaching, he made Lyndell forget her own dowdiness, her fear of revealing too much.

They talked of the war, and he complimented her on the depth of her understanding, beyond that of most of his London acquaintances. They talked of books and the theatre, with Lyndell bringing the marquis up to date with what he'd missed. Politics and the antics of the regent, architecture and the new buildings Prinny was commissioning Nash to build, art and opera, they discussed it all, intelligently and as equals, to Lyndell's delight. And she hadn't given anything away, or had she?

Chapter Seventeen

$\mathcal{O}$n Sundays the upright, moral, God-fearing went to church. Lyndell and Felicia took the gig. The marquis stayed at the inn.

"He knows," Lyndell said, as soon as they were on the short way to the little village of Entwood. There'd been a discussion of the wisdom of the trip, but Lyndell thought it would draw more comment if she didn't attend services. She could go, properly escorted by her maid, and relieve the townsfolk's curiosity, before many were tempted to stop at the inn. She had a black bonnet with a veil, borrowed from Mrs. Bennett, so she felt she could meet any unexpected old acquaintances with safety. It was easier to keep up the masquerade if she could direct the play, as opposed to her dealings with the marquis, who seemed unwilling to follow the script! "I don't know how he knows, but he does."

"Willy swears he didn't tell. He says his cousin is just a 'downy cove,' whatever that is."

"It means he is clever."

"Oh."

Lyndell had to smile, but this was serious. If the marquis made her presence there known, Felicia's future would be doomed. She'd never get vouchers from Almack's, invitations to all the balls. She'd never meet her Beau Ideal, that handsome man who would love her to distraction, and she him, for ever after.

"Please, Felicia, please consider returning home before anything worse happens. Most likely Cheyne will keep still out of regard for your father, so we can squeak through. Otherwise your chances will be ruined."

Felicia giggled. "My chances would be ruined a lot faster if I left now."

When Lyndell took her eyes off the horses, not so chancy a move with Jasper's plodders, the girl was blushing.

"Why, Felicia Fullerton, I believe you are setting your cap for someone!" For an unnamed reason the thought that Felicia might have reconsidered her father's arrangements, now that she'd met the marquis, caused Lyndell's throat to tighten. No, the girl was still terrified of him; Lyndell could swallow again. "Willy!"

"Isn't he the most handsome gentleman you know?"

Willy?

"And so fine and brave. He was telling me how he almost ran away and enlisted, because Lord Richardson wouldn't purchase his commission. Instead he gave up his own wishes to stay back and help manage his cousin's properties. *So* noble, don't you think?"

Happily Felicia was content to ramble on about

115

the myriad splendours of the young lord, with Lyndell only murmuring an occasional "Indeed," or "How true." Felicia and Willy? Yes it might do, if her father permitted it. Richardson wasn't up to Cheyne's weight as a prize on the Marriage Mart, of course, but he was well-to-pass, a cheerful, likeable young fool, and with any luck could keep Felicia out of harm's way. They'd make a remarkably handsome couple, both fair and blue-eyed. Their children would be perfect cherubs . . . and perfect widgeons. The ideal match, if Willy was agreeable.

"That's why I must not leave. Willy said he'd take me home himself, as soon as his foot is healed, and explain to Papa. And I'm almost sure, well nearly positive, that he'll stay to ask Papa's permission if . . ."

"If you have a few more days to work on him! Well, if anyone can bring him up to scratch, you can. In the meantime, don't let on that Cheyne is right. Maybe he's only guessing. And Felicia dear, please do stop smiling at the blacksmith."

The village of South Entwood was hardly big enough to merit a name of its own. Beside the church and the smithy were Patchin's Dry Goods and Mr. Beck's Emporium. Beyond was a cluster of labourer's cottages, and the more substantial houses of the vicar, the doctor, Mr. Beck, and the Misses Pelham—Miss Millicent, who gave music instruction to the neighbourhood children, and Miss Serephina, who did fine sewing. The two prim ladies ran the parish charities and held genteel at-home teas.

Miss Riddley glided past all of them in the churchyard, with just the proper degree of courtesy. A nod, a small bow. Nothing unfriendly, but nothing to encourage familiarity. She was a solemn stranger in her black veil, intent on her devotions, the little maid two steps back. It was a magnificent performance, till Lyndell nearly botched it by almost marching right up front to the Markham family pew.

The marquis was on his hands and knees, but not in prayer. He was searching the innkeeper's apartments. The results seemed to please him or, if not please him, then at least satisfy him, to judge by the smile he later gave Willy, pulling up a chair near his cousin's bed.

"You know, I've had a lot of time on my hands, and I've been thinking about Miss Fullerton. Perhaps it's not such a bad idea after all . . . so I thought, while you are laid up, I might just go on north and get the job done, and fetch you on the way home. I'll leave you Farrow, of course. With that ministering angel who has adopted you, you should do quite well. What do you think?"

Willy was twisting the bedclothes into knots, getting red in the face and stuttering. "But I . . . She won't . . . You can't . . ." His cousin finally took pity on him and burst into laughter, waiting for Willy's sheepish grin in return. "How did you know?"

"You gave it away yourselves, you clunch. The moment you saw the girl you told her you fell. Fell? I couldn't for the life of me imagine why you'd tell clunkers to a perfect stranger." He brushed some dust off his fawn trousers. "I hadn't, at that moment, precisely recalled Miss Fullerton's first name. Then she was so attentive, and you appeared quite taken with her."

"Well, I've known her forever, our fathers are good friends, I told you."

"Forgive me for being a bit slow . . . I had other things on my mind. Where was I? Oh yes. It wasn't in your usual style, cooing over a lass—and a maid at that," said the marquis, ignoring his cousin and pursuing his own train of thought, "which brought to mind the last female I'd heard you mention. Did I say mention? I mean proclaim, and jump to her defense at the slightest insult. That was what our absurd duel was about, wasn't it?"

Willy coloured up. "But I couldn't let you talk like that, not when Fel—Miss Fullerton is such a sweet, innocent—"

The marquis held up his hand. "Enough! Belatedly, I must admit, I did recall your description of Miss Fullerton as a perfect china doll, all guinea-gold curls and blue eyes."

"Wasn't I right? Isn't she the most beautiful, pre—"

"Quite. But more obviously, the chit was no maid at all. Have you noticed how she dresses Miss Riddley?"

"I try not to."

"See? Well, to tie it all up, I inspected her room." When Willy started to bluster about indignities and talking liberties, Cheyne told him, "Don't be a gudgeon. I had to know what she was about, didn't I? You, most loyal cousin, were keeping mum. No, I realise you were sworn, or some such. At any rate, the lady travels light: one bandbox with the initials FF on it, two fashionable muslin gowns, some lacy things I did *not* examine so you can stop scowling at me, a string of very expensive pearls, and a fur-lined cape. A pleasure to travel with, I'd say, without all the trunks and cases women usually tote around. Handy thing to have in a wife . . ."

"A wife? Wes, you're not . . . no, gammon, you're

teasing again, aren't you?" At his cousin's expectant, encouraging smile, he went on: "You don't mind if I . . . That is, Wes, you were . . ."

Cheyne laughed. "No, Willy, as long as your intentions are honourable I don't mind. I'm relieved in fact, and I wish you all the best."

"It's a bit early for congratulations, Wes. Want to see her father, do it all in form, you know."

If the marquis was amazed at Willy's new respect for the conventions he hid it well, thinking only what strange effects love had on its victims.

"There's one more thing, Wes," Willy was saying; "I know that you know about Felicia, and she *thinks* that you know, but could you pretend not to know? You see, Felicia thinks it's the most romantic thing ever, right out of a Minerva Press novel, to be secret lovers." Cheyne cleared his throat; Willy stammered. "No, not that kind of lovers. You know what I mean, Wes."

"Say no more, cuz, the lady shall be allowed her flights of fancy." Actually, it suited the marquis perfectly to have the heiress continue masquerading as a maid. She'd be safer from recognition and possible scandal that way. Compared to what else was going on at the inn, her charade was mere child's play. Which reminded him . . .

"Will, have you ever taken a good look at the landlady?" he asked nonchalantly.

"No, thank the gods. What a fright!"

"But does she remind you of anyone?"

"Only m'sister's dragon of a governess, why?"

"Just a notion I had. Would she seem familiar, do you think, if she had glorious reddish hair with golden touches, and brilliant green eyes?"

Willy was hooting. "Don't tell me you're developing a *tendre* for Miss Riddley, that stick! The only lady I know anywhere near your description is Miss Markham, a real Incomparable, and anyone less like your dowdy innkeeper I've never seen. You know, I think the Markhams used to come from this area. Maybe Riddley's from the wrong side of the blanket, and that's why you see a similarity. Didn't know you were acquainted with Miss Markham though."

"I'm not. It was just a foolish idea, as I said."

However far-fetched, Cheyne's search of those rooms had given him the notion. The clothespress had yielded two sturdy, serviceable gowns—Miss Riddley was wearing a third—and a handful of others in muslin, silk, sarcenet, and crepe. Frocks designed, if he knew anything after two months of footing the bills for opera dancers and actresses, by the finest London dressmakers. Most of the fashionable gowns were in shades of green or a peach-rose, colours to complement coppery hair and green eyes to perfection. There were no boys' clothes here, but Jasper's closet could have held enough. A valise was crammed full of old account books, whatever that meant. In the bedroom where he had accosted the red-haired imp Dell were Miss Austen's novels, no book of sermons, and Miss Riddley's spectacles.

There were two possibilities, as Cheyne saw it. The first was that the proper Miss Riddley shared the room with Delilah. But there had been only one woman in the bed with him; no mistaking that. The other possibility was that my lady innkeeper shared a great deal more with the madcap Dell.

Chapter Eighteen

*W*hen Lyndell was a child, Reverend Smallwood always seemed to direct his sermons at her. Of course he knew all her sins, he lived there right next to God's house, didn't he? The day he raged against pride in his deep voice, he stared right at Lyndell. That very morning in the churchyard, she'd boasted to Cynthia Highte about her new bonnet, when Cynthia had none. And the week Reverend Smallwood shook his fist on high declaring Thou shalt not covet thy neighbour's property, well, that was the week she and Allen Bromley had raided the squire's peach orchard.

The Reverend Smallwood had long since passed on to his final calling, most likely berating the angels for rumpled wings, and a Mr. Teppler had taken his place. The new vicar hadn't the white hair, or the thunder in his voice, and he could not be addressing Miss Riddley when he spoke of the temptations of the flesh. She almost looked around to see if Molly was there, trembling in the back row. She doubted it. When the preacher's monotone droned on about wanton lust, Lyndell let her mind wander. After all, she'd only been sorely tempted twice in her whole life, both by the marquis, and that was finished. He'd shown Miss Riddley the correct deference that evening at dinner, without any sensual overtones. He could act the part of a gentleman, if presented with a proper lady, which Lyndell was determined to be. Dell Riddley was retired. And Lyndell would swear she had done more this week at the inn to discourage illicit fornication than all the Reverend Teppler's speeches on the Serpent in the Garden. The Devil in Disguise meant nothing to Lyndell. As for the wolf in sheep's clothing that Teppler was mumbling about, Lyndell pictured a laughing-eyed rogue in buckskin breeches. She'd already been warned, thank you.

The marquis, meanwhile, was also considering sheep. Mutton dressed up as lamb, to be specific, an ago-old subterfuge. But why in this world, he wondered, would anyone take tender lamb—he smiled— and try to pass it off as stringy old mutton? He was determined to find out.

"I thought I would look in on the dog after luncheon, Miss Riddley. Would you accompany me in case he needs further attention?"

"That is not at all necessary, my lord. The boy Samuel is taking care. Ajax lets him do anything now."

"Still, he's only a lad, and you wouldn't want all our efforts to be wasted?"

What could she say in the face of such civility— No, I don't trust you in dark places? She went, taking the arm he offered to see her over the mud.

Ajax was in fine shape, chasing the sticks Sam'l threw up and down the stable length. The dog dropped the stick the moment Lyndell and Cheyne entered the building, standing stiff-legged a moment, then rushing toward them. He sniffed Lyndell's skirts, gave a vague tailwag, and then practically drooled on the marquis, frisking about him, stirring up the stable dirt in excitement.

"Ungrateful cur," Lyndell called him, laughing. The marquis only ordered "Down boy, you're getting dirt on my Hessians," but he too was smiling. Ajax calmed enough for them to be able to see that his neck was healing, his eyes were clear, and his coat was unmatted and shiny with brushing.

Cheyne looked at Sam'l and said, "You've done a fine job, boy. He'll do. He might even make a good gun dog. What do you think?" Sam'l nodded his head vigorously. The marquis bent over the dog again, his back to the boy. "Maybe we can take him out tomorrow and get some rabbits for Mrs. Bennett's pot. Would you like that?" When there was no answer, Lyndell was about to make the reply, until she saw the marquis frown at her. "Hm?" he asked again, still not facing Sam'l. When the low "yessir" finally came, Lyndell let her breath out, and the marquis stood up, holding his hand out to the boy. Sam'l rubbed his hand on his pants before offering it. "It's agreed then," Cheyne said, his grin matching the boy's. "Now I think you ought to take him out in the sun for some exercise. Build up those muscles again."

"But, my lord," Lyndell asked, "what if the dog runs away? We can't put a tie on him . . ."

"Oh, I think he knows who his friends are now, don't you, Sam'l?" The boy nodded happily and ran out, the dog at his heels.

Lyndell said, "That was very well done, my lord," and turned to follow, but Cheyne said, "Wait," quietly, half-plea, half-command. She waited. If she were a child playing with the sea, running or getting splashed by the waves, it was time to run. But she waited. Cheyne took the four steps separating them, looking into her eyes—the spectacles back in her pocket—or her soul. He slowly reached up and removed the cap from her head and while she stood, almost entranced, he ever so softly used it to wipe at the powder on her face. It was much too late to run. He said nothing; his gaze was intent on her mouth.

Lyndell could no more have moved than she could fly, and Cheyne could have not kissed her as easily as he could have not breathed.

The kiss was joyous and natural, like coming home. Lyndell responded fully, putting her arms around his neck, touching his cheeks, his hair. So much for Reverend Teppler's sermons.

"You're so beautiful," he breathed in her hair, "much too good for Riddley."

"What do you mean? Jasper and I—"

"Come now, precious, Jasper's sister wouldn't have any reason to be in such a disguise, would she?"

Lyndell was coming out of her golden trance. She stepped back, out of his embrace. "You mean, you think . . . Jasper? Oh you—"

He was holding her hands. "Oh no, you'll not slap me again," he said, laughing. So she kicked him. Her soft kid half-boots absorbed more of the blow than his Hessians, and that was fair too, because Lyndell was more furious at herself than at Cheyne. "Ow!" she shouted. Then, "Let go of me, you . . . you brute!"

Sam'l rushed in, launching his small body at the marquis, flailing at him and gnarling. "Hold," ordered Cheyne, letting go of Lyndell and pinning the boy's arms to his sides. So Sam'l kicked him. The marquis's brow was lowering and his mouth was forming into a thin line when Lyndell cried, "Don't hurt him!"

Still holding the boy, Cheyne looked at her quizzically. "Just what kind of ogre do you think I am?"

Spy, seducer, cradle-robber—she didn't get to begin. He shook Sam'l lightly and said, "No more of that, my boots have taken enough punishment. As it is, Farrow will have my hide. It was very brave, lad, coming to Miss Riddley's defence against such a foe, and I admire you for that, but I swear I did not harm her. Did I, ma'am? Tell the boy."

Lyndell murmured, "No Sam'l, he did not hurt me."

"And I never, ever would, I promise." Sam'l nodded, believing him, and Lyndell knew she believed him too. He might ruin her reputation, he might even break her heart, if she let him, but no, he wouldn't purposely hurt her.

Her reputation, Lyndell Markham's, she would guard twice as zealously, and as for her heart, she simply would not permit herself to fall head over heals in love with such a plausible rogue. She simply wouldn't.

"Come, Sam'l, let's go see if Mrs. Bennett needs help with supper."

Intelligent and witty, spirited and sensual, exquisite and exquisitely formed. That was how Lord Cheyne catalogued Miss Riddley, whoever she was. Everything a man wanted in a woman. He still hadn't answered the questions of why a woman, perhaps connected to a noble house somewhat illegitimately, would need to be in disguise, or how involved she was in the other business, the one he'd been sent here about, however secondary it seemed now. The answers would come soon, he was confident, since, in his experience, a man had only to bed a woman to find her secrets. Have her warm and well contented, and she would babble on, if you let her. He hadn't tested the theory recently, Molly suddenly being indisposed toward company, but he was sure of Miss Riddley. The marquis, of course, was forgetting one of his own theories: lose your heart and your head will follow. Not seeing the danger signals, he was dreaming plans for the evening, remembering that kiss, how readily she came into his arms. Gads, what a mistress she'd make.

Chapter Nineteen

"Sir Martin Blazer and Mrs. Blazer? Of course. Rooms Six and Eight. Enjoy your stay."

It was Sunday evening and Lyndell was steadfastly entrenched in her nook under the stairs, in the cap and powder and spectacles. She was not going to be enticed into more indiscretions, not wine before dinner, not another shared meal, not tea after. Nothing. The Marquis of Cheyne was nothing to her, and would stay that way, behind the partly opened parlour door. Not many people chose to travel on Sunday, although Molly and Bennett were kept busy in the common room. So Lyndell was reading Miss Austen by the light of the single oil lamp on the wall behind her.

"Sir Frauncis Hammerly . . . and nephew." The fop in yellow pataloons and a striped waistcoat dripping fobs and chains was indeed Sir Frauncis, the middle-aged, pouch-faced dandy who'd once paid ponderous court to Lyndell's fortune. His nephew was a weak-chinned young man with pomaded curls. Before Lyndell could think of a way to get rid of Hammerly, one of the worst gossips in London, Lord Cheyne casually stepped out of the parlour, leaned against the door frame, and asked if there was a problem. Lyndell stammered something about no available rooms.

"Good evening, Sir Frauncis. Poor Miss Riddley is embarrassed that the inn is nearly filled; the snow I suppose. If I can help though, the single room next to mine is vacant, and your nephew can bunk in with my cousin Willy."

There was an ornate eyeglass fixed to the top of Sir Frauncis's walking stick, and he raised this now to one red-lined eye to peer first at the marquis, then at Lyndell.

"Servant, Cheyne. Miss Riddley, is it? No, no, wouldn't dream of disturbing Richardson. We'll just push on to Ipswich. 'Ta."

When the door was shut behind them, Lyndell gave the marquis a puzzled look of enquiry.

"The nephew, ma'am,"

"Oh? Oh. Oh my. I . . . I see. Thank you, my lord." He bowed and returned to the parlour.

At about ten o'clock Lyndell decided to retire to bed. She had been yawning over the book, and the only new customers to come in were for the tap room. She went to the kitchen to tell Mrs. Bennett to listen for the bell, and she stayed to share a cup of tea before going up.

The marquis followed about fifteen minutes later, according to his own preplanned course. He would wait another few minutes—give her enough time to get settled, not enough to fall asleep—then knock softly on her door. He intended to say he needed to ask where he could hunt the next morning, which was private land, etc. She wouldn't believe his excuse, certainly, but he was willing to wager she would open the door. On the way to his own room the marquis noted that Molly must be back in business: a heavy-set man was entering her room at the end of the corridor. He knew the right one now. Cheyne shut his own door and considered whether he should remove his boots now . . . or later.

Lyndell was sitting at her dressing table, scrubbing the wretched powder and the top layer of skin off her face. She had changed into her lawn night gown, and had brushed out her hair, and had congratulated herself on her noble behaviour. She had vowed not to be swayed by his entreaties, and she hadn't. The only problem, she thought angrily, was that there had been no entreaties! The marquis had not offered her wine, dinner, conversation—or insult. It was one thing to be ready to repulse advances, quite another when the advances did not come. She threw the towel down in disgust. Blasted unpredictable man, didn't even give her the opportunity to say no!

Now that she was wide awake, and in a righteous mood, she decided to see what Felicia was up to. It would not do for her to be so long in Lord Richardson's room, even if the man Farrow was there too. Now whose idea was that? she wondered. Either way, a valet was not adequate chaperone for a young girl's good name. Her virtue, perhaps, but not her reputation. Lyndell put on her wrapper and the white mobcap, just in case.

Felicia was sleeping peacefully. No moral dilemmas there. With her hair in a braid, she looked like a child in Lyndell's candle's light, so Lyndell quietly shut the door behind her and turned toward her own apartment. A movement caught her eye, a man, leaving Molly's room. How dare she, after Lyndell had expressly told her no. And how could she? As the man walked closer, nearer to the hall lamp, Lyndell could see that he was heavy and coarse-looking, with thick black hair and straggle-brows. There were even black hairs growing from his ears and nostrils—disgusting! And why was he still coming down the corridor, past the stairwell? Lyndell didn't want any such scurvy character loose in the halls, so she waited for him to turn and leave. Except that he didn't. He kept coming closer and closer, and suddenly grabbed at her! Before she could even think about screaming, he had one hand over her mouth, and was dragging her back toward her own room. In his other hand he held a knife, right in front of Lyndell's face. She stopped struggling and the knife moved a few inches away. She could see the black hairs on the back of his hand. Dear God, it was the last thing she was going to see!

The marquis opened his door. "What in blazes?" Cheyne did not consider the odds—the attacker had the weight, the weapons, and his boots on, but he also had Miss Riddley. The ex-soldier lunged at the intruder, who spun around, freeing Lyndell though catching her shoulder on the knife edge. She reeled back, holding her upper arm, while the hairy brute turned on Cheyne. The man feinted once with the knife, but doors were opening up and down the corridor. Rather than take on the entire inn, the man shoved past Cheyne, clouting him against the wall, then fled down the stairs. The marquis shook his head to clear it before taking off in pursuit, down the stairs and out the door, shouting for Bennett.

By now Farrow was out, looking for something to

aim his pistol at. Willy was hobbling down the hall in his nightshirt, and Felicia was rubbing her eyes, wanting to know what was going on. Lyndell was still leaning against the wall, blood now beginning to ooze between her fingers, when Mrs. Blazer put her curl-papered head out her door and hissed, "This is not at all what I am used to!"

Lyndell gave a shaky laugh. "Do you think *I* am?"

By the time Cheyne returned, Felicia had swooned twice: once in the hall when she first saw the red stain on Lyndell's arm, and again, right into Willy's thankful arms, when Mrs. Bennett told her she looked like a fallen woman, out in the halls in a ha'penny's worth of lace.

Things were well under control when the marquis entered Lyndell's room. Felicia, more than amply covered in his own paisley silk robe, was hovering over Willy's chair. Willy, from a distance, was giving Miss Riddley—a Miss Riddley *sans* cap, glasses, baggy gown—a very puzzled inspection. Before he could express his bewildered thoughts to his cousin though, he was silenced with a pinch from Felicia, and a whispered, "Later," which the marquis overheard. He would have been amused, except that he was so intent on Mrs. Bennett and Farrow, just now spreading a bandage to Lyndell's shoulder. Mrs. Bennett covered Lyndell with the bedthrow blanket.

"Damn!" said the marquis, astonishment turning to concern as he saw blood-stained rags. "How bad is it, Farrow?"

"Not bad at all, my lord," Lyndell answered for herself. Farrow nodded his agreement. "More a slice than a stab. I don't think he even meant to do it. Did you catch him?"

"No, he got away. He had his horse tied right out front, and took off through the hedges. By the time we could have saddled up, he'd have been long gone."

"Who was he, Miss, er, Riddley?" Willy put in.

Lyndell gave him a wan smile and a nod of appreciation. "Never having seen him before, I haven't the faintest idea."

"You never saw him before?" the marquis asked, giving her a strange look. "The boy Sam'l knew him."

"He did? Did he say who—no I suppose he didn't."

"As a matter of fact, he did. He must have thought it important enough because he came right up to me and said 'Quinn.' That's all, just Quinn."

Mrs. Bennett gasped, but Lyndell murmured "Ah," as if that answered many questions. It didn't for Cheyne and he decided to clear the room. "Farrow, please take Will back to bed before he has a relapse, out in the night. And thank you for your help. Mrs. Bennett, perhaps you would see Miss Felicia to her room"—no one seemed to notice that he used Miss Fullerton's real name—"and then see about some tea, with a little brandy, I think, for Miss Riddley. Thank you." He added, "You needn't worry about Quinn. I doubt he'll return, now that so many people can identify him, and Bennett is downstairs with a shotgun in any case. Farrow, you keep the pistol handy; I'll do the same."

When they were all gone and the door was shut, he faced Lyndell, huddled under her quilt, and demanded, "Now what is this all about? What in blazes did he want?"

Lyndell gave a weak giggle. "I think . . . that is,

it seemed, well, I suppose he wanted to kill me."
And then she was in his arms, weeping against his
chest, and he was soothing her, telling her what a
brave puss she'd been.

"I'm usually not such a watering pot, you know."

"Of course you're not, it's just a reaction to everything," he said, wiping her cheeks with his
handkerchief. "Now come." Without giving her a
choice he scooped her, blanket and all, over to the
chair by the fire, and into his lap. "Tell me what's
going on here. You know I'll help you."

"Yes, my lord."

He gave her his one-sided smile. "Most ladies in
my lap manage to call me Wesley or Wes. 'My lord'
seems a little formal, under the conditions, don't
you think, Miss . . . ?"

"Lynd—Lynn."

"Lynn? It's not—no matter. About Quinn?"

She started to tell him, without making much
sense, so she got up to fetch Jasper's letter from the
pages of her book. Without a second's hesitation,
she climbed back into the marquis's lap before
handing it to him. He pulled her closer and read,
" 'Dear Sister.' Damn!"

"What?"

"You really are Riddley's sister?" Lyndell chose
not to add the "by marriage only"; she saw no reason to lay quite all her cards on the table just yet.
She nodded. "And you really are a respectable female?" She nodded again; he swore again. Dis-
turbed, she questioned. "Wesley?"

He kissed her nose. "I was all set to offer you a
carte blanche; now you're too proper!" He read on
while she blushed.

"It seems Jasper had his fingers in a lot of pies,
smuggling, robberies, but he drew the line at trea-

son. That should save his skin. Too bad he couldn't name the London contact. That would satisfy the War Office. Do you know where Jasper is now?"

"Yes, he's up at King's Mark. That's the manor a few miles back. There's a connexion," she said before he could ask. "Do you think Quinn will go after him?"

"If he thought Jasper would talk, most likely, or if he knew anything. It's too late to warn him now. Quinn would already have been and gone. I'll send Bennett in the morning. But tell me, precious, why would Quinn come after you? What was your part in this, and why the disguise?"

Lyndell took a moment to choose her answer: "I really don't know why Quinn wanted to kill me, unless he thought Jasper had told me something, or he thought I could find some evidence. That was my plan. I was going to wait for the London traitor and trap him."

Cheyne squeezed her harder. "Foolish without permission, my love. Look what it's got you. And you've been tossing every suspicious character out of the inn anyway."

The endearments were being stored away for future examination. Right now Lyndell confided, "That's the good part. Anyone who makes a fuss about staying, unless there is a good excuse, has to be a suspect. So I report him to the authorities and—"

Cheyne burst out laughing and Lyndell could feel it up and down her body. She wriggled closer still. "What amuses you?"

"You do, sweetheart. I'm the authorities!"

It was her turn to laugh. "And I thought you were the spy!"

A few minutes of friendly bantering passed, and

a few not so comradely kisses. Then Lyndell asked, "But what now?"

"Tomorrow," he told her firmly, "you let me handle it. But right now—"

"Ahem." Mrs. Bennett cleared her throat and set the tray down with a thud. She stood there glaring, her arms crossed over her chest, the light of battle in her eyes. All good soldiers can recognise a *force majeur* when they see it. The marquis retreated to the sounds of Mrs. Bennett's final warning: "And you needn't worry, my lord, I'll be sleeping right here, keeping Miss Lyndy safe from harm . . . from *all* harm."

Chapter Twenty

For someone who had been shot at and stabbed, Lyndell was in a remarkably cheerful frame of mind on Monday morning. Her shoulder was stiff, but the sun was out and it was one of those nearly perfect early winter days, clear and bright without a chilling wind. Lyndell's spirits matched the day. For the first time in a long time, she had a feeling of eager expectancy, a sense of something wonderful about to happen, almost like Felicia's excitement over her first Season. Lyndell had been intrigued by the cloak and dagger adventure, like an exercise in logic, before it grew so personal. She had certainly often been pleased over a special ball or spectacular fete, but now she felt that a cloud of tedium had just been lifted, even if she hadn't been aware of its presence. Suddenly she was living a little more fully. The air was crisper, the sky was bluer and she was in—No, she would not call it love, not yet. She would acknowledge infatuation, attraction certainly, but for that final, irrevocable and chancy commitment, no, not yet.

What Lyndell felt was a little kernel inside her, warm and glowing, waiting to burst into full flower. She could cherish that, for now, but not let it grow. The marquis was a rake. It was simple; he could not be trusted, not to be honest or loyal or sincere, and without those qualities, Lyndell could not give herself to any man, no matter what the inclination of the moment!

For much the same reasons, she had not revealed her real identity. If Cheyne was ever to love her, and love her enough to give up those wild bachelor ways, two very separate things, then he also had to love her for herself. Cheyne was not after her fortune, that was not even a question—but what of her social position, her family name? If he could love the plain middle-class Miss Riddley enough to offer for her, Lyndell decided, his love could be trusted. And then . . . If her heart had hands, it was warming them by that little glow.

While Lyndell sat humming, mending linen in the kitchen, the marquis was out hunting, tromping through the woods, teaching Sam'l to whistle. Their noises would scare off any game, of course, but well worth it, considering the boy's laughter. For the very first time in his memory, Cheyne found himself thinking what a pleasure it might be having a son of his own to teach things to, things like shooting and fishing and following tracks around snow-brittled pine trees on a glorious winter morning. The whistling could not interfere, since the quarry whose tracks they were following had been long gone in any case. They traced Quinn's trail through the hedgerows and across some fallow acres, nearing a sizable estate, then through the forest, doubling back to the road, where the prints, heading north, were obscured by cart tracks. Convinced that Quinn wasn't lurking about anywhere close, the marquis gave his full attention to Ajax, blundering through the woodlands, crunching through the ice crust and woofing.

A pointer he wasn't, and it was obvious after the first rabbit that he'd never been taught to retrieve without tasting. Somehow, out of the dog's sheer exuberance, the gentleman's crack shot, and the boy's quick gathering of downed prey, they managed to bag a pheasant, three rabbits and a brace of woodcock, all of which Sam'l proudly presented to Mrs. Bennett, who fussed about congratulating the hunters, fixing them hot drinks, chocolate for Sam'l, mulled ale for the marquis, and reciting aloud possible menus.

Lord Cheyne took a seat next to Lyndell's and recounted the morning's activities: "The dog is a natural hunter. What he doesn't step on, he frightens half to death, then he eats it! We'd be going hungry if not for Sam'l here. Incidentally, we followed the man Quinn's path back to the road. He never went very near that manor you spoke of."

"Yes, that's what Bennett said. He went anyway, to warn Jasper, who is considering whether the inn wouldn't be a better place right now. Safety in numbers, you know. I'm almost embarrassed for him, he's such a spineless gudgeon."

"I'd like to speak to him anyway," the marquis said with a smile that could mean anything. Lyndell thought it the height of ludicrousness for the marquis to ask a Riddley for her hand in marriage, if that was what he wanted of Jasper, but she had no opportunity to discuss it, since the bell at the manager's desk was ringing, over and over.

"I'm sorry to keep you waiting, my lord . . . ?"

"Crowley; I want a room, brandy and hot food, in that order. And who, pray tell, are you?"

"Miss . . . Miss Riddley, my lord, Jasper's sister."

"Didn't know he had one." Crowley looked Lyndell over, then said, " 'See why he never mentioned it."

Lyndell gasped at such rudeness, before recalling what she knew of the Earl of Crowley. He was one of London's prime eccentrics, sometimes of the Carleton House set, when he chose to socialise at all. More often he was found at racing meets, horse auctions and stud farms, where his unkempt appearance and rough tongue were better suited than in the drawing room. Past his fortieth year, he had still not married, the talk went, because no mere female could interest him as much as a sweet-going mare. It was also rumoured that his whole income went to finance his obsession, perhaps, Lyndell thought, even to the point where he would be forced to crime to support his stables.

"We do have a room, my lord, if you want it. The thing is . . . well, have you ever had the measles?"

"Measles? What's to do with measles?"

"You see, we had a family staying here, and the children came down with something, then the maids . . ."

"No matter, girl, just get me a key. I must've had the spots when I was young."

"But, my lord, I . . . I feel I had better tell you that we fear it may be smallpox. So the inn at—"

"Measles, smallpox. I don't care if it's the French pox! I've been riding since sun-up and I'm not putting my arse back in the leather today. That's final!"

He might not worry over his own health, but his horses were another matter. Lyndell was about to create a dire disease in the stables to challenge his determination to stay, when she noticed Cheyne, leaning against the door frame. He'd changed from his hunting clothes into dove-grey pantaloons, a black coat and black waistcoat embroidered with silver. What a contrast between him and the new-comer in his stained buckskins and bulky frieze jacket. Both were tall, well-built men, but the earl merely looked crudely rugged; Cheyne elegantly virile. The marquis was smiling, most likely enjoying her discomfort, and shaking his head. No, don't discourage the earl more, or no, don't let him stay? Drat them both!

."Room Five, and your groom can bed down in the stables. I'll see to luncheon in a half hour in the tap room. Our private parlour is already spoken for."

"Cheyne, eh? I saw his team out back, prime goers, I'll bet. Oh, there you are, Wesley. Had them off Folger, eh? Set you back a pretty penny . . ." And Crowley wandered off, forgetting about his hot bath, his brandy and his key.

"Room Twelve, Lord Dodgett? I'm afraid that room is occupied by a . . . a button salesman. Won't another do?"

"No, no, it must be Twelve! Well, perhaps Four-teen. I'm tracing the path of a certain star, you see, and I come here to check its progress every month. Mr. Riddley understood. Are you sure he's not here? Oh, dear. My experiment, my papers for the Royal Astronomical Society—"

"My stars." Lyndell had to smile to herself; Cheyne was unfortunately still talking to Crowley.

"If it's that important, perhaps I can move the button merchant. Room Twelve, you say? Would you mind waiting in the common room while I see?"

Lyndell flew up the stairs and gave Room Twelve a quick survey, opening the empty drawers and checking behind them, feeling the mattress for suspicious lumps, even tapping for loose floorboards. Stargazing indeed! A likely story for the Duke of Burfield's second son. About as likely as pigs flying. There must be something, but Lyndell couldn't find it. The bell summoned her back downstairs as she was wondering if secret codes could be sewn in the curtain hems. She'd have to search later.

"Sir Hammerly, you're back." That sounded cloth-headed even to Lyndell. Of course the aging macaroni was back, now in a red and gold waistcoat and red-heeled shoes with sequined buckles; he was staring at her through the glass on the top of his walking stick, almost searching for flaws, she felt. "And your nephew?"

"Oh, I sent the dear boy back to school. Too, too tiring. Then my valet developed a putrid throat, so I left him at Ipswich, couldn't travel with him of course. What was one to do? I simply couldn't show my face in London without being dressed properly; luckily I remembered this quaint little inn. So refreshing, you know. Perfect for a repairing lease. I trust there's a room for me?"

Chapter Twenty-one

*W*illy was to be allowed down for dinner for the first time that evening, and Cheyne invited Lord Crowley and Sir Frauncis to join them in the parlour. Felicia had offered to serve, an idea quickly vetoed by Mrs. Bennett, Willy and Lyndell, who together finally convinced the girl that she'd never be able to take her place in Society if she was found out. Besides, she would most likely spill something. The problem was, however, that Molly had decamped for good, dresses, bonnets and all, sometime during the day, before anyone could question her about Quinn's presence. With so many travellers, especially those used to special services, the inn was short-handed, even with the marquis's man Farrow assisting. Lyndell's offer to pour ale in the common room didn't even merit a tongue-click from her old nurse, who simply assumed she'd been teasing. The work was finally apportioned: Bennett would take care of the tap, Farrow would serve the titles, Mrs. Bennett would cook and dish out supper for the common room, Sam'l would watch the stables, Felicia would mash the turnips (the only kitchen task Mrs. Bennett would assign her) and Lyndell would, again, mind the hall desk, and help ferry dishes from Mrs. Bennett to Farrow. So it was that, amidst all the comings and goings, when the parlour door was left ajar, she could overhear parts of the conversation.

"Fine table they put on here. Much better than before." Obviously Lord Crowley.

"You've been here before?" Cheyne's deep tones.

"Too damn often. There's a good breeder an hour north. Hard bargainer, old Eckles, but prime stock. I got my bay colt off him in—"

"Why don't you try some of this hock, Crowley? It's quite fine. What about you, Sir Frauncis, have you stopped here before?"

"Occasionally. On the way to my nevvie's school, of course. But tell me, does the proprietress seem familiar to you?"

Cheyne said no, he was positive he had never seen her before coming here; Willy, a few glasses of wine in him, started: "It's 'cause she's—"

"Related to some of the better families," Cheyne finished. He didn't want Willy blabbing on about Miss Riddley's possibly illegitimate connections with any local noble houses.

Lyndell was thankful to the marquis for protecting her, as it appeared, until Willy persisted: "But she's not just plain Miss Riddley. She's—"

"My dear boy," Cheyne drawled, almost in imitation of the dandified Hammerly's affectations, "if you are finding Miss Riddley anything *but* plain, you'd best go back to bed. The wine has been too much for you."

All four men laughed. Lyndell wasn't quite so appreciative anymore. She positively glared at Lord Dodgett when he came wandering down the hall, heading toward the kitchen.

"If it is dinner you want, my lord, Mr. Bennett will serve you in the common room."

"What? Oh yes. I forgot I wasn't at home, of course. At home I simply see if cook has left me something, whenever I'm hungry. It's much too difficult otherwise, leaving an experiment in a crucial stage, just because others call it dinnertime."

"Of course." Enough of this, Lyndell decided. The gentlemen would be a long time over dessert, then port and cigars, maybe even cards later. And with Dodgett out of the corridors too, she could not miss the opportunity. She signalled Bennett to listen for the bell, then went up.

Dodgett's room was nearest, so she began there. It was much the same as before, except there actually was a telescope set up on a tripod at the window, with stacks of notebooks on the chair. The notebooks really did seem to record dates in monthly intervals, times and distances for various planets, comets or whatevers. It could be a clever device for noting full moons for smuggling, perhaps too clever, since farmer or fisherman knew the times and tides without such equipment. The rest of Lyndell's search revealed a single change of clothes and some books, many in Latin. They could contain hidden messages, for all she knew, but she doubted it.

Hammerly's room was closest to her own, so she saved it for last, certain she could make a dash for the corridor, seeming to be innocently on her way, if she heard anyone approach. That left Crowley's, and Willy Richardson's, of course, now that he was out of it for the first time. No, not Cheyne's own cousin. She opened the door to Crowley's room. What a mess!

She had seen the man carry in his luggage, a satchel and his saddlebags. The stuff must have grown on being unpacked. There were discarded clothes and only barely fresh ones, a sack of sugar lumps and some ancient apples. There was another set of notebooks, and a leather wallet, right in sight, on the dresser with used towels. The man was a fool; the wallet was stuffed full of money—money borrowed, stolen, extorted? The first notebook listed mares and foaling dates, with sires, stud fees and breeders. Another diabolical code!

When she had the second book in her hand, she heard steps on the stairs. She dropped the book and ran. Damn, she was on the wrong side of the corridor. There was Cheyne, helping Willy into his room, and there was Crowley, coming straight at her.

"Good evening, my lord, I was making sure the room was adequate. Is everything to your liking?"

Cheyne was scowling at her, suspicious of what she'd been at. She didn't look at him.

Crowley looked at her though, looked at the door to his room, and said, "So the old maid's still got a race in her yet, eh? It ain't what I'd have bet on, but if you've a mind—"

Lyndell spat out, "Sir, this is not the stable!" and stalked off. Cheyne was smirking, while Crowley muttered something that sounded like "heated-up spinsters."

She opened her own door, turned and slammed it behind her, then locked it. There! She took a few steps across the sitting room toward her bedchamber when a shadow moved and a man came toward

145

her. Oh God, Quinn was back! "Cheyne!" she screamed.

The man said, "Hush, Dilly. It's me, Jasper."

By now Cheyne was pounding on the door. Lyndell took a deep breath, requested her heart to beat less loudly so she could think, and shoved Jasper into the bedroom. She went to the entry and opened the door enough to give a view of the empty sitting room. "I'm sorry, I thought I saw a mouse. Good night."

She could hear Crowley mutter, "Yup, skittish, just like an old mare in season."

"Jasper, what are you doing here?"

"Zounds! Dilly, you look a quiz. What's that? Oh, I thought you wanted me to come. Bennett kept nattering on about your reputation and rakes and Quinn. Did he really try to stab you?"

"Don't you try to tell me you've finally found your conscience, Jasper Riddley, and you've come to protect me, for I won't believe it for tuppence! Bennett said you'd show, for fear of Quinn. Well, you can end it all now. Your spy's most likely here so you can identify him to Cheyne and settle the whole thing. Cheyne says if you do, the other charges will most likely be forgotten."

"Cheyne, huh? Is that how come you called for him just now?"

"He ... The War Office sent him. I'll go fetch him, Jasper, except please remember he only knows I'm your sister, Lynn Riddley."

"Wait up there, sis. How is it, if he's so trusty, he don't know your real name, huh? And besides, what am I supposed to tell him?"

"Jasper Riddley, you have your attic to let! Do you think I'd want anyone to know I'm running an

146

inn, fraternising with smugglers, all in this dowdy rig?" She didn't add the clincher, "And that I'm really related to you," but she was thinking it! "As for what you'll tell him, you'll say which man spoke most with Quinn, or the couriers, and who was here when that messenger was killed, Crowley, Dodgett or Hammerly."

"They're all here at once, and Cheyne too, you say? Damn good opportunity for a hand of faro."

"Jasper!"

"Shush, Dell, unless you want to bring 'em all in here. Listen, I don't know why you'd think I'd know how it was; they all come and go regularly, and Quinn, well, he was always around. I didn't watch who he talked to."

"Don't you have a suspicion?"

"No, and for that matter I can't figure why you'd think the real traitor would come back here. Now that the government's in on it, he'd be a fool to show his face."

"Unless he wanted to finish you off too!" When Jasper whitened, she said she was sorry. "That was mean."

"No, you're right. If it is one of them, and he sees me here, he'll think I'll name him to Cheyne—and I'll be found when the snow thaws in the spring. Better be going."

"Tell me one thing first, Jasper: if you had no evidence, and you weren't involved in this, why did you write to me? What did you think I could do?"

"Oh, I . . . ah . . . I thought you could go to some-one in the War Office, say, and, you know, get them to drop the whole thing. For a favour, like."

"For a favour? You mean you thought I'd—Jasper, how could you?"

"What about Cheyne, huh? You and he—"

"Get out!"

Jasper poked his head out the door, making sure no one was stirring. Then he tiptoed down the hall, boots in hand, and down the stairs. Three doors shut softly after he'd gone: Lyndell's, Cheyne's, and one other.

Chapter Twenty-two

Lord Dodgett paid his shot Tuesday morning and left after breakfast with only his telescope, reserving Room Twelve for next month. He returned about noon for the forgotten suitcase of clothes. Lord Crowley spent the morning in the stable with Cheyne and Bennett, and departed after luncheon. He left rubbing his cheek, finally convinced that Miss Riddley was not ripe for a tumble in the hay. Sir Frauncis was keeping Town hours, sleeping till noon, then requesting breakfast, which was not forthcoming due to rebellion in the kitchen:

"Ham and buns, indeed. If his fancy lordship is so 'dreadfully famished,' he can just lay his own eggs! Who's going to cook lunch, I ask? And serve it, and clean the turnips off my stove top? And who, Mr. Bennett, is going to put my closet back to rights? There's Miss Lyndy nigh murdered in her bed, and now some ... some swine is pawing through my dresses and tossing them all about.

Dirty, that's what it is, and I won't stand for it. You go right into towan, Mr. Bennett, and hire me some more help. Two chambermaids mornings, is it, so I can slave all afternoon and nights while you argle-bargle with every sot in the tap? *And* not keep an eye on what's ours. I know the way back to Islington, I do."

Bennett went into town. It was Farrow, fetching his employer's luncheon of rabbit stew with dumplings, who kindly offered to carry the eggs in to Hammerly, who again was sharing Cheyne's once private parlour. Lyndell herself carried in the coffee and stayed to pour it, a perfectly ladylike service that Mrs. Bennett, even in a pet, couldn't argue with. Lyndell was busy noticing how Cheyne's smile grew, just for her, right up to little gold flickers in his eyes, when Hammerly's drawl caught her attention.

"I always take a walk after meals, so healthy for one's digestion, you know. A brisk jaunt on a sunny winter's day is the perfect thing. Perhaps you'd care to join me, Cheyne?"

"Sorry, I promised Willy a hand of piquet. Perhaps Miss Riddley would like an outing, put some colour in her cheeks." And he winked, behind Hammerly's back, knowing full well her ashen look was due to powder, not lack of fresh air.

"Thank you, but no. With Mr. Bennett off to town to hire new help, I must stay to look after the desk."

She stayed about two minutes. After Hammerly minced out the door, all fussily muffled and mittened and in boots at least, instead of his high-heeled shoes, she raced up the stairs to search his room. She was deciding whether to start on the dresser or the clothespress when the marquis quietly, cautiously, entered. He was not exactly pleased to see her there.

"You little fool," he raged, shaking her at the same time. "What in all damnation are you doing here? Haven't you had enough excitement, almost getting killed? This is not some ladies' tea party, my girl, and I will not have you in any more danger, do you understand?"

"Yes, but—"

"But nothing! I said I'd handle it, blast it."

That was too much for Lyndell. His concern was touching; his high-handed domination was intolerable. "Is this how you intend handling it, my lord, by shouting at me? I suggest we get on with the search instead, before Sir Frauncis comes back and finds us here squabbling like children."

The marquis sheepishly acknowledged her logic, going so far as to admit his ill temper was due to worry over her safety, before turning to the wardrobe, patting down each garment.

Lyndell gingerly lifted handkerchiefs and neckcloths, putting everything back in its precise place. "What of your game of cards with Willy?" she thought to ask.

"Oh, he was teaching Felicia to play piquet. Something about winning all the money now, so no one can say he's after her fortune later."

"You know, then. Do you mind?"

"Mind? I'm delighted. It's about time Willy settled down and made a life for himself. He can't go on just being my heir and nothing else. Especially now."

Now that the marquis was thinking of setting up his own nursery? It was something to think about. Right now, though, Lyndell watched him squeeze the shoulder padding on a jacket. "Wesley?"

"Yes, my love?"

Ah. "This may sound foolish, but could you please tell me what we're looking for?"

"Seals. I thought you knew."

"No, I had no idea there was any evidence here. I just thought it was worth a look. Jasper couldn't have known either; he said last night the spy would be insane to come back."

"So that was the mysterious Jasper. I was hoping so, and not some new beau of yours creeping about at night."

"What, did you think I was like Molly, with gentleman callers?"

"Of course not," he answered, wisely, if not honestly. The thought had crossed his mind, to be instantly dismissed.

Content, Lyndell kept searching: "Tell me about the seals. How many? What kind?"

"As for what kind, stolen and counterfeited, from the War Office. At least three or four, we think. I'm not positive they are here either; I don't think our man would be carrying them around. In addition, the attempt on your life makes me more sure that someone doesn't want you stumbling over anything."

"Yes, but what were the seals here for?"

"It's fairly complicated, and still conjectural, but London pieces it together this way: At first the traitor in London collected valuable information himself. You know, the kind mentioned at parties and discussed at clubs. He located Quinn, who we know had business dealings with the French, to transfer what he learned. Then, our man realised he could find out when couriers would be passing through here with more substantial information—reports, orders, et cetera. He could not simply steal the documents, but he could copy them, hence the false seals ... and hence Quinn's part, besides his role of carrying the stuff to Napoleon, in exchange for the brandy and silk. Quinn or his wife would drug the wine, or get Molly to, uh, distract the courier. It only took seconds to read the documents and reseal them, using the counterfeits. The riders never knew the packages had been tampered with, so the plan went undetected a good long time, I'm afraid."

"The dead courier?"

"Exactly. He must have noticed, or protested, and they had to get rid of him. After that, the investigation showed a great many of the riders would stop here as the last stage before Southwold Barracks. A few finally admitted dallying with Molly. Incidentally, if you are interested, that's why I was ... visiting her that evening, to try to get information."

"Why should I be interested?" Lyndell wasn't going to fall into *that* trap. She'd heard lots of sweet names and sweeter hints. What she hadn't heard, loud and clear, was any kind of declaration. She started checking behind the drawers now. She found a shilling, nothing else. "But if it's Hammerly, and he didn't carry the seals with him, why should they be here? In this room, I mean? I could have given him any room in the place."

Cheyne stopped trying to get the high heels off the red shoes to see if they were hollow. "Damne, what fools we've been! Of course they're not here. And he's certainly too clever to travel about with evidence that can hang him. But he'd have to come back, to make sure they were safe, and not likely to be discovered ..."

"Outdoors!"

"Exactly! I thought it strange that that Bond

Street stroller would crave vigourous activity, much less chance mussing his clothes."

"Yes, the road is muddy and the fields and by-paths are still snowy. It's not a very good day for a walk, not in yellow-lined top boots. Let's go!"

"Let *us*?"

They were well chaperoned: Ajax doing his rambunctious best to muddy the trail, and Sam'l studiously following the tracks as Cheyne had taught him. Just beyond the inn they passed Hammerly coming back.

"Your idea of a walk sounded so enticing after all, I decided to follow your lead," the marquis told him. "Miss Riddley kindly agreed to accompany me so I wouldn't lose the way."

Hammerly raised his glass to examine Lyndell in that obnoxious way of his. She hadn't found the ratty squirrel shawl in Felicia's clothespress, and wasn't about to ask Sarah if it was in the Bennetts' ransacked closet, so she wore her own green cape. Hammerly stared long and hard at it, as if trying to recall it or to remember whether the inn proprietress had been so slouchy the day before. He lowered the walking stick and moved on, with a brief "I trust you will enjoy it," leaving the distinctive imprint of left boot heel, right boot heel, then small circle where the cane made its mark. He should have been easy to trace, but none of the visible tracks they were following had that third impression.

"So the cane is just another affectation, only for the public, I suppose?"

"Yes," Cheyne replied, "just like his drawl. And just like your stoop and those absurd spectacles. You can take them off now, before you walk into a tree. Here," and he removed them for her, taking the opportunity for a gentle kiss. Lyndell motioned toward the boy and Cheyne laughed. "The ideal chaperone; he won't tell anything! But, Sam'l, did you notice the snow on Hammerly's boots? He must have left the road at some point not too distant, so keep an eye out. Here, try Ajax on this." He presented a glove taken from Hammerly's room. Instead of sniffing it to fix the scent in his head, the dog grabbed the glove for a game of tug-of-war, then stood shredding it when the marquis let go, laughing.

The boy and the dog dashed ahead. Cheyne took Lyndell's hand in his, as if it belonged there. It did.

"Wesley," she asked as they walked, off the hard-packed road now and through snow, "are you so sure it's Hammerly? What if it was Crowley or Dodgett, or someone else entirely, who hasn't even come yet?"

"I was not quite so sure until this morning. As for the others, Crowley was sent by Lord Wilkerson to see if I needed any assistance."

"That old reprobate, working for the government?"

"Oh no, my dear. Earls don't work, they volunteer. He's very handy, you know. Gets everywhere, talks to everyone. He's really a fine chap."

"Well, what of Dodgett? He could have stashed the seals in his telescope and no one would be the wiser."

"Sorry. Dodgett is one of the foremost tacticians for the Admiralty."

"That moonling? I can't believe it!"

"You'll have to, pet. The stargazer's a brilliant logistics expert. Advises the entire fleet on weather, tides, windshifts. His loyalty is unquestionable."

"What about Willy, then?"

Cheyne laughed. "My cousin Willy? He hasn't two thoughts to rub together! Whatever made you think of him?"

"I didn't, not really; it was just your suspecting the Bennetts, who practically raised me."

"The Bennetts? I never even considered them. They'd just arrived, for one thing. And Mrs. Bennett is one of the starchiest ladies I know, a lot more moral than the Almack's patronesses!"

"Then you didn't search their rooms last night?"

"Of course not. Why do you always think the worst of me? I wonder, though . . ."

Ajax was barking and hopping around excitedly while poor Sam'l tried to restrain him before the dog obscured the trail ahead. It was not easy, without a collar on the animal, the dog so big, the boy so small, until Cheyne ordered him down. The dog sat, wagging snow all over his back, but he sat. Lyndell and the marquis were able to see where the footsteps circled right around a large tree, before doubling back toward the inn on a path a few feet away. At the rear of the tree there was a hollow in the trunk, and a large stomped-down area. Cheyne looked in the depression, then felt around it with his gloved hand.

"Nothing. But I doubt the seals were here. See how he paced around in back? And there doesn't seem to be a dry spot where a package rested. No, I think this was an old hiding place and he came here out of desperation, thinking Quinn may have moved the seals from the inn before leaving. I'd bet they were supposed to be in Quinn's quarters, Mrs. Bennett's rooms. Hence last night's search."

"But they weren't there, nothing was. And Hammerly didn't find them, or he'd not have come out here. So what now?"

"Now he should have to contact Quinn, unless he already has. He should be getting anxious. Anxious enough to make a mistake. Then we've got him!"

Chapter Twenty-three

"No, Lord Cheyne, you shall not spend the night in my bedroom!"

"What happened to 'Wesley'?" Lyndell and Cheyne were having tea in the parlour alone, and he was quietly explaining his plan. "It's the only way, pet, besides my most favourite wish. And here I thought . . . ?" There was that devilish grin, the one that made her insides feel like pudding. "No? We shall have to talk about it later. For now, it is one thing to use you for bait, quite another to throw you to the wolves. If I hint to Sir Frauncis that you have the seals, and you're ready to go to the authorities, he will have to try something, something you couldn't handle but I could. Therefore, during dinner you will disappear, with everything you'll need for the night. An empty room or Felicia's or mine—no, I wouldn't trust Willy. Either way, you will not be seen in the halls after dinner. If Ham-

merly comes to your room, which I'll leave un-
locked, he'll prove his own guilt."

"What makes you think he doesn't share your
interest in sharing my bed?"

"You would most likely slap me if I told you. No,
he'll be there for less pleasurable purposes, and I'll
be waiting for him. Farrow will be on the alert, and
I'll tell Bennett to keep watch."

"What about Jamison? Shouldn't we notify him?"

"Ah, the captain. I have a feeling he'll know. We
can send for him tomorrow if this plan fails."

"But what if Hammerly sends Quinn or someone
else, another smuggler? Or more than one?"

"You are borrowing trouble, Miss Riddley. Quinn
would not dare show his face, firstly, and secondly,
Hammerly is only expecting to deal with one female. He won't send in the troops. To make sure,
I'll tell Bennett to see that no one else gets up the
stairs. We'll have to make certain anyone seeking
rooms is turned away. The fewer people around, the
safer for everyone."

For everyone but you, Lyndell thought, but she
did not say it.

"How lucky, Signora Fravielli, some of your
countrywomen are staying here too. Sisters of the
Blessed Virgin, I believe. You'll be able to converse
with them at dinner. You can't stay? How unfortunate. I'll give your regrets to the sisters."

"A room, Lord Minhard, for you and your . . . *two*
companions? Room Fourteen is the only one available. I think they'll have removed the bodies by
now."

* * *

"I'm so sorry, Lord Reynald, we have no suite for you and . . . Lady Reynald. Most of the inn is let to the Slovakian National Dance Band. They are practising here before touring London. We do have a small room . . ."

Dinner was stuffed goose and gossip. The marquis skillfully directed the conversation down light, non-personal routes, alternating between *on dits* and sporting talk, for Willy's sake. Willy and Sir Frauncis had almost nothing in common, neither age nor interests, and it was only the younger man's courtesy that hid his boredom and disdain. He excused himself before the port, at his cousin's nod. Then, not having to face any awkward questions from Willy, the marquis was able to come to the point.

"Tell me, Hammerly, do you think old Crowley could be right about Miss Riddley, that she's just a vapourish female, given to imaginings?"

"Did Crowley say that?" Hammerly swirled the wine in his glass, looking at Cheyne through pale, red-rimmed eyes.

"Oh, you know Crowley. He thinks every woman would be better off with a quick toss. But that woman does have some dashed peculiar notions."

"Oh?" The man was good, Cheyne decided; he'd be a hard one to read at cards.

"Yes, she keeps nattering on about some evidence in a courier's death. Something about a spy ring. If it's true, she ought to go to the authorities, I told her. But I don't know, it could all be a hum. You've been in this neighbourhood before. Do you know anything about it?"

"I do recall something of that nature, rather dreadful occurrence, to be sure. Does the lady have the evidence though? You'd look foolish calling in the Home Guard or whatever one does, on a woman's whim."

"Just what I thought! She said something about seals, but she wouldn't let me see them, doesn't trust me, I suppose." It occurred to the marquis, and not for the first time, that Miss Riddley did not, in fact, trust him at all. He had given her every opportunity to unburden herself, to tell him one good reason for the blasted disguise, to tell him just what she was hiding. He felt he was almost ready to accept any excuse she might give, no matter how damning, as long as she gave it. He knew she thought him a libertine and a philanderer; he could cross that bridge with time. This deeper mistrust, the basic lack of sharing, was an insurmountable gulf, a chasm between them.

"Perhaps she just doesn't like men. You know those dried-up shrews."

Cheyne remembered those kisses, and smiled. "Perhaps. Ah, well, I suppose we'll never understand women. What do you say to a hand of piquet to while the evening? Fine. I'll just look in on Will first. He was looking a trifle peaked. Be back immediately."

What Cheyne was doing, actually, was offering Hammerly a chance to stew. The marquis didn't want to give him too much time, or a chance to flee altogether, just enough to come up with the most likely solution: stealing the evidence. Cheyne also wanted to warn Willy and Farrow that the trap was sprung, to be on guard. He brought a book of poems of Sir Walter Scott into Miss Riddley, safely, but not serenely, locked in the maid's room.

"Thank you. How kind. Did you tell him?"

"Hmm?" The marquis was lost. Here was the real

Miss Riddley, whoever she might be. The soft reddish curls, the glowing skin, an emerald robe making her eyes appear even greener. Maybe it didn't matter, after all.

"Sir Frauncis—did you hint to him that I had the seals?" She spoke a little louder, breaking his reverie.

"Shh. Yes, and he seemed so indifferent he's either a masterful actor, or thoroughly innocent. I had better go keep him occupied, and you had better stay in this room, my love, or it will be bellows to mend with you. Do you understand?"

"Yes, my lord," she answered demurely, then added, "Please be careful."

He winked at her before turning to go back down.

Lyndell paced. Then she read a poem from Cheyne's book, trying to think of him reading it, wondering which were his favourites. Then she paced some more. This was absurd! It could take hours, most likely would, before Hammerly took any action; it wouldn't be until long after all the lights were out, and the men were still downstairs. And how was Cheyne to get into her room without Hammerly seeing or hearing him? Felicia had not even come to bed, so Lyndell had no one to talk to, to tell of her doubts and fears. What a stupid plan!

As it turned out, it was not so much the fault of the plan, as the failure to account for all the players. Cheyne had overlooked Hammerly's hole-card, the joker of the deck, and had misdealt the queen out of the game. The marquis found himself playing solitaire, while Lyndell gambled at Hazard.

When Felicia finally came to bed, she was carrying a note addressed to Miss Riddley. "I found this on the table in the hall. Who is it from?"

"It does not say," Lyndell murmured, distracted. What it did say was: "If you ever want to see your brother Jasper alive, be at the King's Mark coach house at one hour past dawn, and bring the seals. Come alone." There was no signature, but none was needed.

Lyndell's first thought was to go straight to the marquis. But no, he had told her to stay. Her second thought was that if she got a message to him in time he would insist on going with her, or instead of her, putting himself in danger again. The hours she had already spent worrying over him convinced her to keep her own counsel for now. She knew the coach house—of course, she did—and how it was situated on a rise, away from all other buildings, with the grooms' chambers upstairs giving an open view of anyone approaching. No, stealth could not save Jasper; nor could a whole troop of rescuers, not without the seals. If she rode to Jamison to fetch a company of soldiers, to surround the coach house and demand surrender, Jasper would be killed and named as the traitor, with no way to prove otherwise. Then again, what if that slimy Jamison did not believe her, would not bring his men? No, she would have to do it herself, with or without the dratted seals.

There was something of the night's tension in her resolution, and something of rebellion against her recent thoughts of giving up her hard-won independence. And there was something else, a lesson she had learned long ago, taking a horse out of the stable without permission. That mare had been too big for a twelve-year-old Lyndell, but her pony was no more challenging than a rocking horse, and she would just show Bennett and those Riddleys how well a Markham could ride, see if she didn't. It had taken a great, painful while for her to mount, the stepping block still not giving her the full height she needed. Then she had stood on the fence beams, but the horse moved and she was on the ground. Her next effort sent her right over the mare's back, and onto the ground again. Finally she had been up, for two minutes, until Bennett whistled to the horse. Insignificant penny's weight on her back or not, the mare was going to have her lump of sugar. The animal had headed for the gate—and Lyndell had headed for the ground. The mare had gotten her sugar, Lyndell had gotten the wind knocked out of her, and then a thrashing from Joshua Riddley, tears from her mother, and a moral from Bennett: " 'At'll teach you to bite off more'n you can chew." It didn't. What it taught Miss Markham was not to get caught, and not to fall off.

She mightn't have the seals, but what Lyndell did have, besides her determination, was money and prestige. She had not met the situation in many years where her family name and a full purse could not work wonders. As much as she might deplore the hypocrisy and insincerity of aristocratic trappings, they were handy when dealing with prigs like Hammerly, to whom social standing and wealth meant everything. She also reassured herself with the fact that while a dead Miss Riddley might cause a local stir, a murdered Miss Markham would create a furor that Hammerly could not hope to avoid.

She no longer had to worry over Cheyne's well-being, and she felt confident of her own. As for Jasper, he would be safe until she could get to him at dawn. Lyndell acknowledged that concern for Jasper himself had not been a large factor in her early actions. But as much as she might wish to have him drawn and quartered, she would do her utmost to see no one else harmed him! The fear of scandal no longer mattered either. If the Marquis of Cheyne could not accept poor Miss Riddley with her weasel-principled brother and no dowry, then Miss Markham would just retire from society altogether. She'd live at King's Mark and raise pugs, and Aunt Hardesty and the others would recover as soon as a new scandal brewed. Of course, Lyndell did not really like the pop-eyed dogs, but for now she would concentrate her worry on waking up on time. As soon as Felicia's breathing softened, Lyndell pulled open the curtains, so the morning sun could come in. The bed looked too warm and soft, so she piled blankets around her on the chair, then drowsed a bit. She woke the first of many times with a trembling start, hearing a pug's asthmatic wheeze. Gads, who would have thought Felicia snored? At least there was no chance of oversleeping!

"Fine game, Hammerly. You almost had me, that last hand. Think I'll turn in now. What about you?"

"Oh, not so early. I'm used to Town hours, don't you know. Didn't realise it was so dashed boring in the country. What *do* the locals do? I think I'll stay by the fire here; at least the brandy is good."

Hammerly's plan suited Cheyne, who had time to go to his own room, fetch his pistol, put Farrow on the alert, and position the chair in Miss Riddley's room to face the door. He settled down to his uncomfortable vigil as Hammerly called out to the barkeep for another bottle. Cheyne, of course, could not hear the dandy offer Bennett a glass or insist on it, as a token of his appreciation for excellent service. And Cheyne, upstairs in Lyndell's bedroom, certainly could not see the white powder that trickled into Bennett's drink along with the wine.

Chapter Twenty-four

The note had said one hour past dawn. Was dawn sunrise or first light? Lyndell did not know. As soon as it was bright enough to see, she splashed some cold water on her face and put on her dress. She had not brought any of her own gowns to Felicia's room, so the brown bombazine would have to do, but she combed her hair till sparks flew and pinched her cheeks to offset the fabric's muddy tones, then covered it with her own emerald green cloak before creeping down the stairs. Bennett was asleep at the hall desk, his head on the ledger. He'd always tried so hard to protect her, poor dear, Lyndell was glad she didn't have to lie to him. The inn was still, except for his breathing, and every creaking step she took toward the front door—away from the light-sleeping Sarah—sounded like a thunderclap to Lyndell's ears. The door moaned like an actress in a Cheltenham tragedy, but Bennett didn't move, nor was there a challenge from the kitchen.

Lyndell was out, watching her breath make smoke in the air and hurrying back toward the stables, when Ajax barked. "Hush, you miserable beast," she shushed him, running up to him and pushing the dog back through the stable door. His bark was about to change to a welcoming yelp when she shoved her leather glove into his mouth. She led him to the loose box which had become his bed, hoping to calm him back to sleep, or at least keep him occupied. Ajax ran into the stall to begin shredding the glove, and Lyndell followed. There was Sam'l, sitting up on a straw pallet, rubbing his eyes. His blankets were all about, showing where he'd spent the night, instead of the nice room they'd fixed for him in the grooms' quarters overhead.

Lyndell smiled and told the boy to go back to sleep, she was just out for a walk. Then she bent to pet Ajax once more, telling him to stay there in his nest of old blankets and what looked a great deal like that old grey squirrel-lined shawl. So that's what Felicia had done with the ugly thing, given it for the dog's bed, wretched girl, rather than chance having to wear it again. What if someone came to claim it? But no, it had not been found upstairs in one of the inn's rooms, nor even in the common room; Lyndell remembered Mrs. Bennett finding it in the Quinns' closet, the only garment there, the only thing left in a closet that was later ransacked! The shawl was already a hotel for fleas when Hammerly searched the clothespress, when he examined the hollow tree. No wonder he thought Lyndell had the seals!

The lumpy seams ripped easily, the fur parting on its own as Lyndell tugged. Four, five, no, six seals fell into the straw, and a stick of dark red wax. Lyndell gathered them up into the pocket of her cloak, then reconsidered and pressed one into Sam'l's hand. "If I am not back in an hour," she told the boy, "give this to Lord Cheyne and tell him I've gone to the coach house at King's Mark. Bennett will know where to find him. Do you understand?" The boy nodded quickly. He understood, fine, but would he tell anyone? Here she was, entrusting her life to a boy who'd said less than ten words this week! Lyndell didn't even know if he could figure an hour's time. Well, Hammerly still wouldn't kill her, not with one seal missing, and not if she offered to pay her and Jasper's way out, if she could return for a bank draft. She touched Sam'l's cheek one last time before leaving to pick her way between the hedges on the path leading to the manor. Lyndell turned and waved at Sam'l, still in the stable doorway. She took the final step into the hedge gap—and there was Captain Jamison, just on the other side. Lyndell's heart practised the quadrille in her throat for a moment.

"What . . . what are you doing here?" She noticed he was smoking a thin black cheroot.

"One of my men was at the pub last night." He jerked his head toward the inn; two stringy blond strands came unoiled. "He heard something about the murder and missing evidence, so I came to investigate. What about you, hm? What's Jasper Riddley's beautiful sister—if you are his sister—doing out so early? Meeting a man, sweetings? It wouldn't be Jasper, would it?"

His smirking presence made sense; she hadn't been downstairs last evening to hear the talk, but the captain was at least in full uniform for the first time, sword and all, and no soup stains on his front. Yet where were his troops, and why was he lurking (the only word that suited the ogling, droolly toad) in the shrubs before sunrise? Besides, even if she could bring herself to trust him, the note had been specific: "Come alone." She answered his insinuations with a cool "What if I am? What business is it of yours?"

"Hoity-toity is it? You weren't so high in the instep when you were done up like an old spinster. Why don't we see if you can be a little friendlier to an old soldier, hm, sweetings?"

He took her arm and started to lead her away, still on the King's Mark side of the hedges, but toward the road. She was going to be late if this buffoon continued. She pulled away from him, toward the home wood path.

"I believe you mentioned government business, sir. I suggest you get on with it and let honest citizens go on their own way. Good day."

She did not get far before his hand was clamped on her arm. "You just don't know what you're getting into, sweetings. I tried . . ." He twisted her arm behind her back and propelled her closer to the road where two horses were standing, held by a hugely fat, dark man—Quinn! She started to kick and scream, which earned her a filthy rag stuffed in her mouth, making her almost retch, and a sharp upward jerk on her arm, nearly causing her to faint from the sudden pain.

"Anyone see you?" Quinn was asking.

"No one but the boy."

Quinn snickered. " 'E's nobut a dummy. I seen to that. Let's go. T'boss be waiting." Lyndell was hoisted up sideways into the saddle in front of Jamison, firmly pinned there by his arms reaching around her for the reins. A slap on the face and a warning, "That's just a taste, if you don't sit pretty," kept her from struggling.

Lord, what had she gotten into now? Jamison was obviously in the plot, and how foolish of her not to have seen it in his watery, shifty eyes! Someone had to warn Hammerly or Quinn when the couriers were coming, and someone had to cover up any murmurs among the soldiers about delays or altered wrappings. And someone, someone in a position of authority, had to be turning a blind eye to the smuggling operations. Jamison. Lyndell wondered if Cheyne knew or suspected. Then she wondered if he would come. In time.

They were passing the open lodge gates of King's Mark, unchallenged. The gatehouse looked abandoned, but surely the grounds staff would be up and about ... or old Tyler or the kitchen maids. Anybody!

Jamison and Quinn turned off the carriage drive long before reaching the house; Lyndell could clearly glimpse the tall red-brick chimneys. They picked their way through the ornamental shrubs, finding the short cut to the stables, almost as if they owned the place, she thought bitterly. They gave the empty stables a wide berth, going back in the trees to circle around to approach the carriage house from the wooded side. Not a soul was in sight, as opposed to all those times when she had had to acknowledge ten curtsies and seven head bobs just getting from the house to the stable. Never again would she let the place be so deserted, even if she had to adopt some indigent relations. They rode right into the carriage house where two horses stood harnessed to the dusty old family coach, not used in years. A few other vehicles, one without wheels, huddled in the gloom. Lyndell did not see Hammerly before she was dumped off Jamison's horse and into Quinn's hairy clutch, to be dragged to the equipment room. Quinn faily reeked with the scent of garlic and sweat, and he grunted as he shoved her across the room toward Jasper, who had blood dripping down his forehead. Diccon sat, tied up, in another shadowy corner.

"Swine," she spat out, along with the foul rag, knowing she was insulting every pig in England. She was bending over, mopping Jasper's head with her handkerchief when Quinn growled, "T'boss says to check'n make sure she's got them seals." He grabbed at her while Jamison pawed at her body, for "places of concealment," he told her, and sniggered.

Jasper jumped up, behind Quinn, and brought both fists down on the fat man's head, shouting "Get your filthy hands off her!" Quinn released Lyndell, shook his head, setting his black-whiskered jowls to flapping, and clouted Jasper above his ear. Riddley went down, almost out.

"Here," Lyndell said, flinging her cape at Jamison, "they're in the pocket, you dastard," then stooped to cradle Jasper's head in her lap. "Thank you," she murmured. "That was foolish, but sweet. I didn't know you had it in you."

Jasper managed a weak grin. "Neither did I."

Jamison tossed back her cloak, without the seals, slamming and bolting the door behind him and his apelike cohort. Lyndell was starting on Diccon's ropes when she first heard Hammerly's voice, without its Tulip's drawl.

"What took you fools so long?" he was shouting. "We've got to get them and the carriage out of here now!"

"Ah, y'know t'capting with a pretty face."

"A pretty face? Miss Riddley? What cork-brained notion do you have now, Jamison?"

"Cork-brained, is it? I'm thinking I've got a better use for Miss Riddley than sending her off a cliff in a coach with your precious evidence."

Hammerly snorted. Lyndell could hear his footsteps coming, the bolt being slid back. She stood up and faced the door defiantly.

He was wearing lime-green pantaloons and a purple waistcoat strewn with red roses. He held his glass-headed walking stick in one hand, and a pistol in the other. And he was cackling. After an instant's shocked silence, the wrinkled, purplish lips had opened in a squawky chortle, and it went on and on, almost insanely. Lyndell shrank back against the wall where Jasper was propped.

"Ah, how kind the fates can be," Hammerly finally got out. "Your servant, Miss Markham. Here we were, taking the last, desperate measures, and salvation was sitting around the corner."

" 'Ere now, Gov, let's just get on w'it like we figgered. Make it look like they was headin' for the coast with the goods 'n some kegs, 'n end this bloody enquiry for good."

"Plans have changed, you fool. This lady represents one of the largest fortunes in the kingdom. The very building we're standing in is hers! And we don't have to harm a hair on her pretty little head, either. We just marry her and it's all ours. She can't testify against her husband, and I'd see that she wouldn't. Oh it's too, too perfect."

Lyndell was too relieved he wasn't talking about overturned coaches and cliffs to concern herself with his ravings, but Jamison was paying closer attention. He was getting redder in the face, and breathing in raspy gulps. "What makes you the one to get the girl and the fortune, hm? You were all set to kill them, if not for me. And what about Riddley?

172

And him?" pointing at Diccon. "I say we send the two of them over, like we planned, and *I* get the woman. We can live like kings in Italy, if what you say about her money is true. Then neither of you has to worry about a thing."

Hammerly cackled again. "Stubble it, Jamison. You'd only waste the opportunities. With the Markham connexion I can reach the highest circles; no doors would be shut to me. While you—Pah, you'd never amount to anything but a half-pay officer gambling away your wife's dowry. You're nothing but low-born scum, Jamison, so don't get ideas above your station."

"At least I don't wear corsets and high heels like some stinking Nancy, you damned Macaroni." He lunged at Hammerly, ready to throttle him. "Why, you—"

The shot was deafening in the small room.

Chapter Twenty-five

"*I* will never, ever, marry you." Lyndell spoke quietly, determinedly, in the silence that followed Jamison's body slumping to the ground and Hammerly's pistol, now empty, clanking on the floor. Instead of fainting, as she wanted to do, or even casting up her accounts like Jasper in his corner, or being shocked witless, Lyndell found perfect clarity, and a last smidgen of courage. The man was a complete bedlamite, and she had to stall, to bargain, to delay whatever obscene plan he devised.

"Tongue-valiant to the end, eh? I think you'll change your mind, though. What if that was the only way of keeping Jasper alive, eh? Not that I relish having a rowdy innkeeper for a brother-in-law, mind you, but he does seem to hold some place in your affections. Too bad I didn't recall the connexion earlier, although I can understand you not bruiting it about. Relatives in trade, my dear, are not at all the thing."

174

"I'd rather have my relations earning an honest living than leeching off society," she countered, only to be met with, "An honest living? Jasper? How naïve you are. But you will marry me to keep him safe, for now."

"I'd rather die first."

"That, too, can be arranged, my dear. After the ceremony, of course. No, you'll be the perfect bride—rich and beautiful—and the most compliant of wives, one way or another. Too bad about Jamison, I could have had him tame you. That was his type of diversion, you know. Ah, well, there's always Quinn." Lyndell couldn't help the shudder that rippled through her. "Quite. And you needn't think your family will protest either, for I'll make sure they know there'd be an epic-proportioned scandal, without their cooperation. One way or another, Miss Markham, you'll be well and truly compromised."

"Sorry, old chap," came a deep voice from the doorway, "but I've already had the pleasure. Innocently, of course."

The marquis stepped into the room, a pistol held nonchalantly in his hand as he surveyed the carnage. "Miss . . . Markham? Are you injured?" he asked, his dark eyes strained with anxiety. When Lyndell shook her head, he muttered, "How fortunate for you, Hammerly." He nudged Jamison's body with his boot, wrinkled his aristocratic nose at Jasper, still retching in the shadows, and returned his attention to Hammerly, while keeping a loose aim with the pistol, for Quinn's sake. "I have three men outside, all armed, plus a boy and a particularly nasty dog. How easy shall you make this?" He could have been offering for a dance, for all the emotion he showed.

Hammerly also stayed remarkably cool, merely nodding his acknowledgement of the odds. Perhaps it wasn't so remarkable, Lyndell decided, considering he'd just killed a man without an instant's hesitation. "Swords?" he asked, as if debating between a waltz and a quadrille. What a peculiar ritual! The marquis gave a half-bow and stepped over Jamison, pulling the captain's sword from its scabbard and slicing the air a few times to feel its weight.

"You mustn't!" Lyndell cried, but the marquis only nodded and told her, "It's the only way." He handed her the pistol, having to wrap her limp fingers around it, and squeezing them in his. He gestured toward Quinn. Lyndell moved the pistol in Quinn's vague direction as, horrified, she watched the marquis drag Jamison's body toward a wall. She knew Quinn was edging to the door, but her eyes would not leave the trail of blood smearing along the floor. When she did look up, Quinn was at the entrance. Maybe she could have pulled the trigger if he was moving toward the marquis, but away? Her hand fell to her side.

There was a clatter of hooves and a shout, barking—then a shot. Willy's voice called out, "Got him, Wesley. You couldn't have done better." Cheyne's lips tightened into something between a smile and a grimace as he bowed once more to Hammerly.

Sir Frauncis twisted the eyeglass on his walking stick and pulled a wickedly thin blade from the cane, then attacked. No bow, no salute, just a mad lunge. Lyndell gasped, and this time the pistol came right up to center on the dandy's waistcoat, but the marquis parried easily. The lighter blade had the advantage of speed and manoeuverability, and in the hands of a master might have threatened the heavy sabre, but it was the marquis who had the agility, the stamina and the skill. There was some metal screeing against metal, but no real contact before Hammerly was clutching his side as blood poured over his fingers, the blade slithering to the floor.

And then Farrow and Bennett and Willy were all there, untying Diccon, holding a pad to Hammerly's wound. "You could have killed me easily," he gasped. "Why not?"

"That's why," said the marquis, his eyes on Lyndell, "though you'll never understand." He was taking the gun from Lyndell before she dropped it. "Give it to me, my girl. That's how Willy lost a toe."

"I say, Wes, you swore not to tell! What do you wish done here now? Can't just leave bodies strewn about, you know."

Cheyne had his arms about Lyndell's shoulders and was leading her to the door, but he paused. "No, I suppose not. Bennett, if you could fetch the magistrate and that discreet doctor of yours, I'd be grateful. I'm afraid you'll have to stay here till then; Farrow, see what you can do to keep Hammerly awake till I get a confession signed by him. And you"—to Diccon—"I don't know your name, but get Riddley cleaned up, will you?"

"As for you, sir," he addressed Hammerly, "I'm tempted to let you free once I have the guarantee of your confession, and your promise to stay abroad. Jamison and Quinn were guilty enough to satisfy Whitehall." Hammerly grimaced, but acquiesced. "I would like to avoid that scandal you mentioned." Another nod. "Yes, I thought so, especially when you'll remember how very, very easy it would have been for me to kill you . . . or would be in the future, if ever a mention of Miss Markham's name passes your lips. You do understand, don't you?"

"Yes, yes, a pox on both of you. Just leave me." He waved one lace-edged wrist at them, then he gave the ugly cackle again. "But you'll get yours too. With the magistrate and the doctor and the servants and the stable hands—you'll have to get married. B'God, cotched at last, a cold bride and a reluctant groom! You'll find what hell is, soon enough."

"Perhaps" was the only answer as Cheyne gently ushered Lyndell out. She hesitated this time, whispering to him until he turned back. "One last question, Hammerly. What did happen to Quinn's wife?"

"They were going to France . . . smuggler's boat. Revenuers started firing . . . men all ducked down but she jumped overboard. Couldn't swim. Too, too stupid, don't you know?"

Lyndell was too numb to reprimand Felicia for flying into Willy's arms while a strange man in an old-fashioned wig harumphed in the background, and she was too exhausted to wonder at the girl's dainty sprigged muslin and the pink ribbons in her curls. It was unseemly, of course, but Lyndell was simply beyond caring. Mrs. Bennett gathered her up, exclaiming at the state of her dress. It was covered in blood and dust and horse hair, with the hems sodden from the snowy walk home. Lyndell was trembling with cold and fatigue—and relief—when the marquis handed her a glass of something hot and, in his usual politely commanding fashion, requested Mrs. Bennett to see to a hot bath and a warm bed for her.

"Come, poppet. You'll feel better in no time. And

I'm going to burn that awful dress." Sarah fussed; Lyndell would have protested, but the marquis raised the hand he was still holding and kissed it tenderly. "Go now, I have some details to take care of. I'll see you at luncheon."

Lyndell had a few details of her own to take care of once she was warm and clean and rested. The first was putting on her prettiest dress, a green shot-silk with ecru lace at the low neckline, the high waist and the scalloped hem. It was a trifle too fancy for ordinary daywear, but not for this extraordinary day.

Her next business was with Jasper, and it was simple: how much and how far. Riddley still had a greenish tinge and was not really up to complicated negotiations, so he settled for less than Lyndell was prepared to offer: a tidy advance on a monthly allowance and passage to America—if he left that week.

"Damn generous of you, Dilly. You won't regret it."

"I already do. Leave today and I'll double the cheque."

The victory celebration seemed to be in full swing in the tap room, with bottles and huge platters set on the long tables. Sam'l, declared to be the real hero for his timely warning to Cheyne, was ensconced atop the bar, grinning, while Diccon was recounting his tale, an abbreviated version, as edited by Cheyne. The audience consisted of locals like the doctor and old Jake, the usual lunchtime customers, plus Lord Crowley and some recently arrived, well-dressed strangers, including the bewigged man seated between Felicia and Willy. Sarah and Bennett and the kitchen girls were busy serving, trying not to trip over Ajax who was adding his noise to the clamour of toasts and cheers and rattled dishes. The only one missing, besides Jasper, was the only one she wanted to see, so Lyndell turned to leave. It was Willy who shouted that his cousin was waiting for her in the front parlour, if he hadn't paced a hole through the floor yet.

"You are so beautiful, Lynn."

"Lyndell," she said, smiling, still standing by the door, noticing how handsome he looked in his dove-grey breeches, the diamond stickpin in his cravat.

"Ah, the ladylike Miss Lynn, and the hellion Dell, the most perfect combination a man could hope for."

And suddenly she was in his arms, pressing as close as she could so their hearts could touch.

"Gad, I am never going to let you go again!" he murmured between kisses, telling her of his horror at the peril she had been in. Then Lyndell expressed her own remorse, at lying to him about her name. "At first it was because of Jasper. Not that I was ashamed he worked for a living, but that he was so spineless. And then . . . then I wanted to trust you, but . . ."

"But what, precious?"

"But you'd never said you loved me!"

"Loved you? I have loved you from the day I met you! Every independent, persnickety ounce, every little curl on your beautiful head. I even loved you when I thought you were a spy. I was ready to run off to Australia with you!"

"But Wesley, you've only known me a short time! We don't really know each other. What if it's only midwinter's madness?"

"Do you doubt your love for me, darling?" he

asked seriously, her face cradled in his two hands. The answer was in her eyes, so full of love and wonder that he grinned and said, "If you're so worried, we can have a long engagement: two weeks. That's all I'll wait, I swear."

"But how can I marry a man I've never even danced with?"

"Another big problem, my love." And he started humming "te-dum-dum-de-dum," and swirling her around the room. They ended up on the sofa, laughing, then embracing again, so enrapt that they didn't hear the banging on the door. They did manage to look up when the bewigged man stomped into the room and glared at the marquis.

"Disgraceful, I tell you, sir, absolutely disgraceful. A respectable chaperone indeed! Your uncle would be horrified at this whole episode. I can only hope, for his sake, that you're finally going to do the right thing."

As soon as the door closed behind him, the marquis kissed Lyndell again, that seeming like the right thing to both of them. In a few moments Lyndell remembered to ask, "Who was that man anyway?"

"Felicia's father, Lord Fullerton. Uncle George's good friend and prospective in-law. Tell me quickly, do you have any such dragons in your family?"

"Why, are you trying to back out already?"

"I'll show you how far I'm backing." And he pulled her down on top of him, their whole bodies in fiery contact. "Dragons, griffins, sphinxes. If you've got them, I'll love them. Except maybe not Jasper ..." he teased.

"What about King's Mark? Will you love that also?"

"Of course. Our second son will need a home too,

won't he? But, sweetheart, if you are worried about my usurping your place here, don't be. I've been off to the wars, remember, so you'll have to teach me about managing. You'll have to help take over my estates, for our firstborn, and third and fourth . . ."

"Hmm. Wesley?"

"I am beginning to mistrust that tone of voice. What bee have you in your bonnet now, pet?"

There was, indeed, the tiniest seed of a doubt, not in her heart, but in her mind, planted by rumour and nurtured by Hammerly's vile tongue and Lord Fullerton's good intentions. She thought that if she didn't get rid of it now, it would grow and spread, like a weed choking out her new-found joy. "Wesley, I . . . that is, you aren't just marrying me because I have been compromised, are you? I don't care about the scandal at all, and it was mostly my fault in any case, so you don't really *have* to marry me."

"Yes, I do, darling," he told her, smiling tenderly, "if I ever want to see the sun shine again, or know how velvet feels, or be this happy the rest of my life."

"Sorry, Lord Wilton, the inn's shut down, temporary like. You might say it's closed for renovations."

PASSION
&
ROMANCE
FROM
RACHELLE
EDWARDS